THE

SECRETS

THAT FOLLOW

PAULA MARIE

Printed in the United States of America
First Printing 2019
First Edition 2019
ISBN: 978-0-578-61326-0

10 9 8 7 6 5 4 3 2 1

I dedicate this book to my daughter Brooke who has taught me more than I can ever teach her including how to love unconditionally she has brought me more joy than I could have ever imagined. To my husband Don who is the love of my life and my soul mate.

TABLE OF CONTENTS

PROLOGUE

On a crisp fall morning in Southern California, a slight breeze swept in from over the ocean and seagulls flew overhead. Paulina stepped into her Mercedes Benz, the lowlights in her blonde hair sparkling in the sun. In a striking below-the-knee cobalt dress that matched her bright blue eyes—which were somehow inviting yet distant—and cream-colored heels, Paulina was a stunning woman for forty-two years. In her younger days she'd been a real show-stopper, drawing every gaze when she entered a room.

Paulina was on her way to work. She was a real estate agent, highly respected in her field, and specialized in high-end properties. She worked solely on referral within her network.

After many years in the business, she was able to handpick the clients she wanted to assist. On this particular Thursday she was meeting with a client who lived in her neighborhood, a sophisticated woman in her early sixties who was recently widowed. She had decided her house was too large and did not feel like home anymore. As Paulina approached the circular driveway and noted the decorative waterfall and grand gated entrance, she understood why this was one of the most expensive homes in the neighborhood. And as she got closer, she felt the unpleasant twinge that always arose in such moments: a reminder deep in her soul that she didn't belong there.

Paulina lived in one of those places that you see in movies and hear about in celebrity stories but that most people can only dream of inhabiting. Rolling hills and trees line a perfectly kept road into a lush, private, gated community where the homes are all perched over the ocean, each one custom made and unique; an understated elegance is inherent in the air that embraces you and reminds you this is a special place to live.

Most of Paulina's neighbors were retired, formerly physicians, attorneys, celebrities, or trust fund babies who never worked a day in their lives. The wives had been soccer moms who spent their days at the gym with a personal trainer, and now they relaxed at the spa, traveled, and entertained. Paulina was one of the very few women who actually worked. People assumed that she worked for the fun of it; they would never have believed that someone in their neighborhood worked to earn money that they needed, or for that matter that they ever really "needed" money. After all, this was Bel Air Estates in La Jolla, and if you lived there you had more money than you could spend. But then again, things aren't always as they appear..

CHAPTER 1
THINGS AREN'T ALWAYS AS THEY APPEAR

I walked up to the door and lifted the heavy brass knocker. As it hit the custom alder door, the substantial thud reminded me where I was and the caliber of the home I was about to enter. When the door opened, I couldn't help but notice how fit the woman behind it was. She smiled and gushed, "Hello, you must be Paulina? I'm Sandy!" Her tight skin reminded me that I was overdue for a laser treatment and that I probably looked a little tired. I sucked in my belly and stood up straight. She wore a pale blue jogging suit that fit snugly and showed off her toned body. One of those women who never had extra weight around the waistline, just a perfectly flat stomach. I always wondered if they starved themselves to look this way or if the last tummy tuck was that impressive.

Sandy invited me in, and as we stepped through the foyer and into the formal living room, I took in her decorating style. *This one will sell.* After many years in the business, I knew within a few minutes whether the home would sell and how quickly. I also could intuit the price it would sell for and, within a few more minutes of talking with the seller, how easy the process would be. I was very good at my job. As we chatted about her home, I complimented Sandy on her exquisite style and did a quick calculation in my mind of the sales commission—$660,000. *Not too bad… "not too bad"?* What an interesting thought. Over the years, I had realized that the more money you make, the more money you want or need in order to feel successful.

Sandy quickly signed the paperwork and invited me over for a happy hour the coming Saturday with a few of her friends. Since her husband Charles had passed away six weeks prior, she knew it was time to move on in her life—sell the house and move closer to her children in San Francisco. She planned to purchase a home there and live there half the year. The other half, she would travel abroad. At the age of sixty-two, it was time to visit Europe again before she got too old. The life insurance proceeds, along with the sale of the house and the trust, would provide more money than she could spend in her lifetime. I accepted the happy hour invitation, flashed a winning smile, and told her I was looking forward to working together.

As I walked away, I worried, *What am I going to wear?* Always the same thoughts crept in: *Will I fit in? Will they know that I am not one of them?* But I'd gotten proficient at dispelling these thoughts as quickly as they arrived. I jumped in my vehicle and cranked the music. I sang the Rolling Stones' "I Can't Get No Satisfaction" loudly as I drove home, riding the high I always got when I landed my next deal. It was a feeling that I'd become addicted to.

Saturday morning as I sipped my coffee with almond milk and enjoyed the ocean view from my deck, I mused over what I'd wear to happy hour that afternoon. I decided on my teal Michael Kors dress with designer heels, which were higher then I liked but made me look taller and thinner, therefore justifying the way they pinched my left foot. I'd finish off the look with a diamond tennis bracelet and diamond earrings. I wore my hair extensions too; they looked so natural that no one had noticed them. Thanks to them, my hair fell to the middle of my back and bounced in a slight wave. Overall, the look would work for today. Before I left, I poured myself a glass of wine. It was only three—a little early for wine—but I had learned that having a glass before a social engagement helped me be more fun and made the persona I had created for myself a lot easier to keep up. I was certain that no one ever guessed I was an introvert and very shy in crowds.

I finished the wine and brushed my teeth, then added a stroke of lip gloss and headed out. As I approached Sandy's home, I noticed the long line of cars down the driveway and into the street. There was a sign that read *Valet Parking*, so I decided to wait in line for the service. I was not walking in those heels. *Wow, this is quite an elaborate neighborhood happy hour...* was my first thought, and my next was that this was a great chance to network. So I checked my clutch to make sure I'd brought a few business cards. Then I remembered I didn't have any and didn't need them; I would naturally pick up as many clients as I wanted just by being there. People would look at me and see whom they wanted to see. They would assume that I was just like them and immediately feel connected to me; they would want to sell their home through me based on their assumptions of me. As I gazed around at the smorgasbord of pricey cars I thought to myself, *Interesting what people choose to believe.*

The valet attendant smiled nervously at me as he opened my door. He was an attractive boy around twenty years old and was clearly impressed at his day's clientele. He took my vehicle, and I headed for the front door. I happened to look over my shoulder and notice a man in the valet line behind me, just getting out of his car. I couldn't help but mark that his car was an older model; it may have been a Cadillac, but older and not very impressive looking. It was remarkably out of place. I did not want to stop or stare, so I continued in the house alone, confident with my signature smile. Sandy turned, smiled, and said, "Hello, Paulina. Welcome!" Several of her guests greeted me with a smile. I headed for the bar and ordered a glass of Veuve champagne. I preferred wine but decided this was the classier option. The champagne kicked in quickly, since after all it was my second drink in the past hour; so, as I started to mingle with neighbors I recognized, the chat came naturally. I worked the room, my most charming mode switched full-on.

After a while I strolled out to the pool. I saw the man from the valet line. After a furtive glance I was certain I'd never met him before. We caught each other's eye and I quickly smiled. I turned away and begin to chat with Phil, a long-time resident who made an appearance at every neighborhood gathering without fail. It hadn't even been a minute before I felt someone next to me, and I looked over. It was him.

He looked into my eyes and said, "Hello." It was the type of look that goes straight through to your soul. It was very unsettling; I felt as though he were looking through my facade. His dark hair was longer than that of most men his age, and his eyes were a steel blue that seemed to see *everything*, if you know what I mean. He was around thirty-five and extremely fit. He wore a crisp white shirt, beige slacks, and leather loafers that were not overly expensive. He had a casual but self-assured vibe about him that was very sexy. The thing about a genuinely sexual man is that the very energy he possesses is sexually charged and impossible to ignore. It will throw even the most confident woman off her game. I myself was caught off guard.

I heard myself say, "Well, hello there," which I regretted immediately. It was an odd greeting.

He just smiled and said, "I'm Blake."

Of course you are. Hot guys never have common names, never Tom or Joe. Always something like Blake.

Our interchange was cut short right there, as several people approached us and one started talking to me about the real estate market. When I turned around a few minutes later, the man was gone. He seemed to have left the party. By now I was three glasses of Veuve in, and I knew from experience that was my limit in a business setting. I made one last round to say goodbye and thanked Sandy for a lovely party. As I waited for my vehicle outside, I couldn't help but look around again for the guy or his Cadillac. Not seeing him, I went home.

Back on my private deck, I poured another glass of wine and got into the hot tub. Overlooking the ocean and situated so that no one could see me, it was entirely private, my favorite spot. I slipped out of my dress and climbed in naked. I never wore clothes in it unless I had company. As I soaked, my mind traveled to the man with the steel-blue eyes. I wondered, *Who is he? Is he a friend of Sandy's?* He seemed so different from the crowd, and his car and clothing did not fit the Bel Air Estates vibe. I was curious and intrigued. I found myself feeling slightly sexual, which was strange, because I had not felt that way in a long time. After a couple more glasses of wine that I didn't need, I went to bed thinking of the mystery man.

CHAPTER 2
MOMENTS THAT CHANGE YOUR LIFE

The crack of the thick yellow belt was thunderous and threatening. He towered over me and my two siblings and snapped it in our faces as a taste of what was to come. I ducked under my sister's arm and hid, the way I always did, and she pulled me close and said, "It will be okay." My brother tried to be tough and act like he was not afraid. As we waited for our punishment to begin, I blacked out the way I always did so that I never really remembered the details.

My mother Bethany was a beautiful woman, the kind of woman that could have had any guy she wanted. She only chose the wrong type, though. She got pregnant at age sixteen and her parents disowned her. They took in her newborn child but sent her off on her own. Basically, they wanted to start fresh with the baby and gave up on her. A wild child, she dated many men, but when she met our dad, she was in love at first sight. He was gorgeous and his name was Preston. He looked like Elvis Presley and had a sexy bad-boy vibe that Bethany adored. They started dating, and soon they moved in together. At first, all was good: they had fantastic sex and partied hard. He had some odd jobs, so they got by. He seemed exciting and full of potential; she believed he would come up with a brilliant idea that would support them forever. But after my older sister Patricia was born, all began to change; he would go out at night and not come back until late, very drunk. Shortly Bethany was pregnant again, this time with my brother Paul. Things went from bad to worse. They lived in a small run-down house. The relationship was strained and they could barely make ends meet. Bethany still loved Preston more than anything in the world, though, and she hoped things would get better. She started using birth control and looking for work to alleviate their struggling. One month after getting on the pill, to her shock, she was pregnant again—this time with me.

As fate would have it, I arrived unplanned and unwanted. By now my mother and her sexy bad-boy husband were on the rocks. He was becoming more and more distant, and his drinking had escalated. He would go out almost every night and come home after 2 a.m., if at all. She was suspicious that he was having an affair; financially, she was utterly dependent on him, and they were falling behind on their bills.

One wintery Saturday, Preston started drinking early in the day. My siblings and I were watching TV when we heard a scream; I ran to my mom's room and saw her lying on the bed. He had punched her, and she was almost unconscious. It was the most terrifying moment of my life; all of the times he had hit us with the belt did not compare to this. I thought she was going to die right there on the bed. I felt so helpless, a skinny five-year-old girl who had no idea what to do. On this day, the day when the physical abuse against my mom began, I changed forever. A small voice in my head that repeated and repeated, "You have to get out of here," sprang into existence. At just five years old, I knew there was a better life. I knew I would have to find a way out of this life and into that better one.

Patricia, on the other hand, seemed to accept that this was the way life was and tried to make the best of our situation. She always tried to protect me. Paul was introverted and hard to read. I believe that, as the boy, he felt responsible to do something to help. He would talk about the things he wanted to do but never actually did them. After all, he was just a child too. Over time, each of us found our way of coping and processing our circumstances. Mine was always the same: *I have to get out of here. There is a better life.* I also knew that I never wanted to be dependent on a man. I knew it at a very young age. I would not grow up to live in fear and feel trapped, like my mom.

CHAPTER 3
THE CHANCE ENCOUNTER

I rose early on Sunday morning with a slight headache from the wine and champagne, prepared my coffee, and headed out to the deck. On especially beautiful mornings like this one, the view still took my breath away. I decided to take my spin class in my state-of-the-art exercise studio, and then had some prep work to do for Sandy's listing. Many real estate agents of my standing hired assistants, but not me. I had learned a long time ago that other people were not dependable and just let you down.

After my workout and a few hours of work in my office, I went down for a walk on the beach. I needed to clear my head after all the paperwork, and it felt good to be outside. As I approached the shoreline, I noticed a person in the distance standing on the sand; not moving, just staring out at the waves. I put in my headphones, started a playlist, and enjoyed the fresh salty air as I walked. Getting closer, I was surprised to see that the person staring out at the water was him. The mystery man, Blake. First I jumped, and then I didn't know what to do, so I awkwardly kept walking by, even as he turned to look at me. Oddly, he started walking in step with me, not saying a word, just walking. He had a slight smile on his face and, like before, that overpowering sexy vibe that filled the air. You would have to be dead not to feel it.

My music was still playing. After he had not said one word after a few minutes, I took out my headphones and said hi.

Blake smiled and looked right through me again. "Good morning beautiful. Did you sleep well?"

I was speechless. *Who is this man that is hitting on me?* I was not naïve; it was evident that he was most likely an opportunist here to benefit from a wealthy single woman living in the neighborhood. I was a survivalist, and no amount of sexiness was going to allow him to take advantage of me. I laughed and said, "Who are you?"

He grinned and challenged, "Who are *you*? I don't think you have introduced yourself?"

"I have to go." The words just came out, and the next thing I knew, I was jogging. Blake stopped and watched me go. I did not stop until he was out of sight. I was breathing hard and feeling rattled and off balance. There were very few people who could make me so nervous, so off my game.

I walked back home the long way to avoid any chance of running into Blake again. As I approached my front door, I stopped short and peered around, then I shook my head thinking, *He doesn't know where*

I live. I'm just overreacting. I went inside, poured myself a glass of ice water with fresh lemon, and went to sit on the deck to collect myself.

It wasn't long before I noticed someone in the distance again. A man headed into the water, slowly throwing off his shirt and pants on the beach. I watched him undress down to his underwear, a pair of black boxer shorts which were cut perfectly to show off his sculpted body. His leanness was complemented by a natural tan; he looked like a surfer with his tousled hair and fit body. As he jumped into the water, I stood up to stare harder at him and then decided to get my binoculars. I usually used them for whale watching. A closer look confirmed that the man was Blake.

CHAPTER 4
THE ESCAPE

A s a child, I learned the art of survival. I knew that my home life was not like any of my friends'. I also knew instinctively that it was best to keep it a secret; people do not want to know that you are living in abuse and poverty. One, it makes them uncomfortable, and two, they judge you. They would like to be compassionate, but they really can't. Humans just aren't wired that way. Armed with this knowledge, I became a pro at hiding my reality and coming off as a "normal" kid. I did okay in school—not great but good enough to get by. I stayed out of trouble and blended in.

One hot summer day when I was fourteen, I stopped by my house with my friend Cynthia to pick up some clothes for a sleepover at her place. I stayed there a lot. Her mother liked me and did not seem to mind me hanging around. She was a single mom who worked a lot, and I kept her daughter company. Cynthia and I entered my house when my father happened to be mid-rage. I was horrified. Cynthia had never seen this part of my life, nor had I told her about it. He was screaming and throwing things in the kitchen, threatening my mom.

When he saw me, he yelled, "What the hell are you doing here? Why don't you get the fuck out of here? GET OUT!" I just looked at Cynthia and said, "Can I move in with you?" She looked scared and said, "Yeah." So I ran downstairs to my room and grabbed everything I could as fast as I could. My heart was racing. I shoved clothes, shoes, and my favorite poster into a bag, and then we went back upstairs. I looked at my mom, and she looked at me. I said, "Mom, I'm moving out." She did not say a word. I walked out and never came back.

Cynthia's mom Jan was not home when I carried all my stuff into their place. It wasn't much, just a couple of bags of clothes and shoes, but it was all there. I was scared that she wouldn't want me there full time. I was there most days anyway, but this was different. Jan was a hard-working person and made enough to provide a small two-bedroom, one-bathroom condo for herself and her daughter. They had enough food and lived a simple lifestyle. I knew she tried to be a good mom.

Jan came home from work at 7:00 p.m. After dinner I was loading the dishwasher and looked at her and blurted out, "Can I stay here?"

She looked up from her book. Jan was always reading a book; she loved romance novels. "Of course."

I hesitated. "I mean, can I stay forever?"

She laughed and said, "Sure, but you have to do your laundry, and you have to do it right."

Living with Jan and Cynthia was a shift in my existence. I felt safe for the first time in my life and found happiness in little things like cooking and cleaning. I wanted to help as much as I could. For her part, Jan never judged me and never asked any questions about my home life. As Cynthia and I grew up over the next year, we started to experiment with drugs and alcohol, just having fun. Some of our friends were trying hard drugs and having sex, but not me; I only smoked pot and never had sex. The voice in my head told me when and where to stop and how to be responsible. Looking back, that seems strange, but since there was no one to guide me or give me any advice as a teenager, it had to come from myself. I worried about my mom, sister, and brother still living at home. Though the youngest, I was the first to escape.

Within the next year, though, Patricia followed suit. She was sixteen at the time. She moved in with the family across the street, who felt sorry for her and took her in after a violent episode from my father left her crying outside one evening.

Not long afterward, my father met another woman he wanted to move into the house, so he kicked my mom out. After all those years of being trapped and living in fear, she was free to go. So she and Paul moved into a small apartment.

A couple of more months went by, and Patricia and I rented an apartment on our own. We lied about our age, dropped out of high school, and got full-time jobs. We worked together at a local sandwich shop, which was close enough to the apartment that we could walk to work. She was seventeen and I was fifteen, and we were living on our own. Looking back, this should have been scary; we were just children with no money, no car, and no support of any kind. But after what we had been through, our new life was fun.

After a couple of years working odd jobs, I was able to buy my first car from a friend's husband it was an older model dodge. He had put fancy tires on it and installed a loud stereo. He sold it to me for $800 and allowed me to make payments. I was on top of the world as I cruised around in my very own ride.

The small voice in my head encouraged me to find a better job. I had experienced a taste of independence, and I wanted more. So I looked at all my options, which were not very many, and decided on beauty school. Patricia thought it was a good idea and signed up too. Fortunately we were both able to get a grant and go for free. One year later, we had our cosmetology licenses and went to work in the salon business. I was an above-average stylist—not the best, but what set me apart was a natural ability to connect with people. They liked and trusted me, and to my surprise I found them telling me things which they afterwards said they felt like they could never tell anyone. After building a solid clientele quickly, I was making more money than I ever had before, and in another year, I decided to get my own place. Moving into my first solo apartment was the most exciting day of my life. I felt so proud and successful to be able to afford it. When I'd furnished it with garage sale scores I loved my new place. Life was good.

After five years of working at the salon, the small voice in my head spoke again, encouraging me to open my own salon. I wanted more. I had saved $5,000 in a retirement account, and that was enough to cover my start-up costs. The space I found to rent was formerly a salon, so there wasn't much to do to spruce it up and open for business. I loved the challenge of starting my own business. Several years went by, and business was so good that I had to hire a few stylists.

I was living a comfortable lifestyle but feeling a little bored. One day a client of mine was chatting away and mentioned offhand that she had a new job working for a new home builder. She was selling houses and loving it. Something clicked in my brain. *I could do that!* The idea stuck with me until I resolved to look into it.

It wasn't long before I was sitting in a model home, trying to sell a house. I'd been hired by an unattractive man around forty-five, balding and overweight. His name was Bob. He was the kind of man that repulsed me, but he found me attractive, so he gave me a shot despite my lack of experience. On my very first day in new home sales, I knew it was what I wanted to do. I knew I could sell houses; I could feel it in my soul. I'd never been more sure of anything in my life.

So I got my real estate license—which was not easy for me. I studied hard, harder than everyone else in the night classes I enrolled in. I was completely determined to pass the exam, but also very afraid that I wasn't smart enough. My father's words played over and over in my head, just like they had when I was in school: *You are a dumbass. You are worthless. You will never amount to anything.* My lack of education always made me feel insecure, and his voice did not make it any easier; but I was resolute and studied night and day while still working at the salon and at the model home.

The day of the real estate exam, I showed up fifteen minutes early. In a room full of other people getting ready for the exam, my heart pounded and I felt light-headed. I took my seat and tried to calm my nerves before the clock started. It was going to be a long four hours. When time started ticking, my heart and mind raced with each new question. I could barely concentrate and started to panic. *What if I fail?* I reread questions twenty times, frozen, unable to think of answers. Around me, people were working quickly through the pages. After about an hour I was able to answer a few questions with certainty, but my concentration was barely there. Another hour passed and several people got up to leave as they finished. At that point, I was not even halfway through; I kept reading and rereading the questions and slowly answered a few more. Larger numbers of people started to flock out of the room as the next hour passed. The room became almost empty, and I was not even close to the finish line. I closed my eyes and said a prayer: *Dear God, I need your help. You know how hard I have worked for this and I don't want to blow it. I honestly do not think I can come back and try again. I have to pass this test. Please help me. Amen.* Then the room was deserted. I looked at the clock and saw that I had twenty-two minutes left. Strangely, I started to calm down and tick off the questions. I went back to the beginning and reread every one, changing some of my answers. I stayed until the clock ran out, then took a deep breath and walked out.

The results of the real estate exam are available immediately. If you pass, they do not tell you your score, only that you passed; but if you fail, they reveal your score and let you schedule a "retake." I walked to the front desk of the now empty building and stared at the girl across the counter. She was young, maybe twenty-one, and seemed to have a bit of an attitude. She glanced up at me briefly, then glared at the computer for what seemed like an eternity, then examined her brightly painted fingernails. "You passed."

I could have leapt in the air. High on life, I celebrated as I drove away from the testing center. I felt like I could do anything in the world at that moment. I sold the salon for $8,000 to a stylist who worked for me. I didn't get a very good profit, but I just wanted out. I was so excited to start my new career.

So, at age thirty, I entered the world of real estate.

Chapter 5
Not Just Any Open House

I planned an open house the following Saturday at my new listing. Sandy readily agreed to it since she was planning to visit her daughter in San Francisco that weekend. I knew very well how to throw an open house for a home of this caliber; I phoned my on-call caterer and florist and started working on the invitations immediately. My network was extensive and consisted of actors, models, plastic surgeons, dentists, and even a few celebrities. The home was one of the most expensive in the area, with a list price of $20,000,000. The houses in the neighborhood ranged from $15 to $25 million. When sold, it would be the most expensive home on my record. The stakes were high, and I was not about to fall short of this opportunity.

All week I worked on preparations and sent out custom invitations to agents for the stars and everyone on my VIP list. I went shopping for a new outfit and decided on a blue Ralph Lauren skirt that fell just below the knee and fit me perfectly: it showed off my long legs and just enough skin to be sexy but not tacky. I paired it with a white silk blouse and striking heels.

Saturday morning arrived, and I prepared my coffee and settled in on the deck to enjoy the view. I was undeniably nervous as the thought that I always tried to avoid crossed my mind: *How did I get here? I don't fit in.* As always, I dismissed it and decided to go for a run to totally clear it from my head. I grabbed my workout clothes and headphones and within minutes was on the beach. I couldn't help but glance around to see if Blake was there, but there was no sign of him. I was relieved; it would've been the last thing I need this morning. After my run, I felt much better. I jumped in the shower and prepared mentally for what could be the biggest day of my life.

CHAPTER 6
OPPORTUNITY KNOCKS

After receiving my real estate license, I quit working for the home builder and applied to some real estate companies. The job with the builder provided good experience, but there was too much politics going on and Bob was always hitting on me. I was very picky when it came to men and rarely dated. That's not to say I had no relationship experience; I had had a few boyfriends over the past decade. I knew I was an beautiful woman and could get almost any man I wanted. But I always felt very distant and didn't trust men—or anyone really, for that matter. I often wondered if I was even capable of falling in love.

I decided to interview with two well-known real estate companies. First, I went shopping and bought a professional-looking black suit. I was nervous; I had never been to an official job interview like this. I walked into the first office and was greeted by a heavy-set bald man who seemed uptight and in a hurry. We sat in his personal office and he proceeded to ask me questions starting with, "Tell me about yourself." He fired question after question at me, and I could not wait to get out of there. I left feeling like I might have made the wrong career choice after all.

I walked into the second interview not quite as anxious and more unsure whether I should even be there. The receptionist asked me to have a seat and offered me something to drink. I smiled and refused politely, sitting down. Within a few minutes, a gorgeous man walked around the corner, smiling from ear to ear—actually, his energy was so high he was basically dancing towards me. He looked me in the eye and said, "Hello Paulina, welcome to Remington Homes! I'm Cody Remington."

I was taken aback. I had heard of his company (everyone had), but I didn't expect him to be so young and good looking. He had to have been only around twenty-one, very young to own such a successful company. We went into a conference room, and he began with, "So, do you want to sell houses?" I smiled and said yes, and told him about my meager experience in the business thus far. He leaned back in his chair and looked at me for a minute.

"You'll make about seven to eight thousand per month, and you will work a lot. The hardest part of this job is keeping up with the level of work."

I laughed out loud. "Seven to eight thousand, come on!" I thought he was full of bullshit. That was crazy money.

He looked at me straight-faced as his smile slid off his face, and he said, "It's true. Would you like to come on board?"

I paused for a few seconds as he looked at me. Then I heard myself say yes, though I sounded like someone else. He asked me zero questions about myself; all he did was tell me how much I would make and offer me a job. He had no idea who I was. What had I gotten myself into?

CHAPTER 7

THE ILLUSION

I arrived at the open house early, as I always did, in order to supervise the caterers and florists. I made sure all the lights were on, the music wasn't too loud, all the waterfalls and fountains were running, and all the blinds were open. I brought a video of the grounds composed of drone footage that I would play on a loop on the large TV in the great room. All was looking good. Sandy had followed all my directions correctly in preparing her home. I loved working with smart clients who had style and understood things the first time around; the early years of my real estate career were quite different, as I'd worked with all price ranges and my clientele was quite diverse. The lower-priced homes were much more challenging to close, and the commissions were small.

The open house would run from twelve to four. At 11:45, I stepped into the ladies' room to freshen up. As I touched up my lipstick and powder, I couldn't help but notice the lines around my mouth. I had not had a facelift or any real work done on my face—

only Botox—but maybe I would consider it. Through the window, I saw a car pulling up to the house. It seemed my first guest had arrived.

The front door opened to reveal a stunning woman. She was probably around thirty and looked like a model—tall, with waist-length dark hair and deep brown eyes. She took in the foyer quickly and then reached out her hand to me and said, "I'm Chelsea. May I look around?"

"Of course," I replied. "Can I offer you a glass of wine or chilled lemon water?"

"No, thank you," she replied and started to walk towards the wing with the master bedroom suite. I always walked with my guests and preferred to give a tour, but it was clear Chelsea preferred to observe on her own. I allowed her to step into the north wing, and then I joined her. I knew Sandy would want me to remain with the clients as they toured her home. I pointed out the custom glass doors that opened to the deck outside, and Chelsea glanced and followed my urging to check it out. The deck was made of glass and gave the impression of walking directly on the ocean's waves. She paused for only a moment to take in the sight and then turned away. I suggested we tour the kitchen and west wing, but she said, "Thank you for your time. Good day."

As she glided away, I looked outside and noticed her ride was a limo. Could she have been an agent previewing for a celebrity? I decided not to waste time trying to figure it out and moved back into the kitchen to await other guests.

Several former clients stopped in next. They were on my VIP list, though they weren't currently in the market, as they might know someone who was. Networking was so important, and, with these crowds, simply priceless. By 3:15 p.m., they had all left. I was freshening up the drink and food stations for any stragglers when I heard the front door open once more. I turned to greet the newcomer and saw Blake standing there. Startled, I managed to say, "Oh, hi."

Blake looked even better than I remembered. Unlike the last time I'd seen him, he looked sophisticated. He was dressed in a lightweight blue silk suit and expensive dress shoes. I have learned to always observe people's shoes; they reveal so much about their wearer. He flashed that sexy smile of his and looked straight through me with those steel-blue eyes.

"Are you here to see the house?" I continued. I had not invited him, so it was strange that he'd showed. *There's no way he can afford this house, why would he come?*

He smiled and said, "I would like to see the view from the deck, if that is okay."

Again, I wondered why. All my years in real estate had taught me not to waste one second on buyers who can't afford the homes they are viewing. I paused and then agreed anyway. I had to stay until four, so I would make the best of it. I led him out to the deck saying, "It is quite a view!" He passed me and walked to the edge, and began staring intensely at the ocean. I came to stand beside him, and we both paused, taking in the view.

Then I felt his hand touching my waist. It was the softest touch I had ever felt; he was barely there. Next he leaned in and brushed my neck with his lips. It was slow and erotic. I stood frozen, caught entirely off guard. He reached his hand down and slid it slowly up underneath my skirt, stopping when he got to my mid-thigh. Bringing his face to mine, he kissed me slowly. It was a slow, sensual kiss. I couldn't move. Then he leaned toward my ear and whispered, "I'll take it."

My mind was dizzy and racing at the same time. *Take what? What is going on?* I wanted to run, but again I was frozen and weak all over. He moved away and added, "I'll be in touch." Then he walked out the door and was gone.

I was still reeling from the experience when the door opened again. I jumped to see Sandy. We both looked surprised at my reaction. "Oh! Hi, Sandy," I greeted her, pulling myself together.

"How did it go?"

I had lost track of time; the open house was long over. "G-good," I stuttered. "I mean, great! We had several prospects stop by. I'll follow up and give you a full report on Monday."

The caterers were busy cleaning up and breaking their setup down. I thanked Sandy for allowing her home to be open and left. I was still shaking and sweating during the drive home. *What just happened? Who is this man, and why am I feeling this way?!*

CHAPTER 8
THE TURNING POINT

My first day on the job as a realtor at Remington Homes was intense. I arrived on time with no idea of what exactly I was supposed to do. I had no real experience. I didn't know how to use a computer or fax machine or read a map, and I barely knew how to use a cell phone. The only real work experience I had was in salons, and that was quite different. On top of it all, I had a horrible sense of direction and was not a good driver. But what I did have was a burning desire to be successful, the ability to read and connect with people, and a lust for money.

Cody worked with me every day. He would take me on listing appointments. We would get in his red Corvette, and he would drive fast. I felt alive when I was with him, and I loved to watch how people would do whatever he wanted them to do. They would sign any paperwork, no questions asked. He taught me a lot about the real estate business and seemed to take a particular interest in me; and I was attracted to him, despite the fact that he was significantly younger and married. He was also Mormon, so there was even less of a chance of us connecting sexually, though I thought about it often. I did not believe in affairs with married men. There are plenty of men in the world, so why choose one who is unavailable? I worked sixty hours a week learning everything I could, and after one month Cody put me on the floor. The "floor" was where we would take calls and get leads. The real estate market was on fire at the time, and the phones were ringing off the hook. I soon found I was a natural and clicked with people almost immediately. I made a few sales right off the bat, still with no real idea what I was doing. I was high on the possibilities and loved the energy that Cody and his office staff displayed. I had found my passion!

One day a call came in on my line. It was a man who sounded older and spoke straightforwardly. He said he was looking to buy about ten investment properties and wanted an excellent realtor. My first thought was that he wasn't for real and probably wouldn't qualify for our services. It goes without saying I had trust issues which originated in childhood; I tended to think everyone was full of bullshit until they proved different. This man's name was Jerry Newman. I asked him whether he had been pre-approved for a loan yet, and he replied no, that he would likely pay in cash. This was even harder for me to believe. But I offered to set up an appointment to go over his qualifications and criteria at my office anyway. He agreed.

It was a Friday at 3 p.m. when Jerry walked in. I had been on the phone all day without a lunch break; my blood sugar was low, and I was not feeling or looking good. I invited him to the conference room. Jerry was in his sixties, short and overweight and graying. He walked slightly hunched over and briskly, as though he had somewhere to be. He seemed calm and pleasant. I asked him to explain his criteria, and he replied: "I will leave that up to you, you're the expert. I want ten rental properties that will be a good investment for me." I told him our in-house lender would have to qualify him, even if he was paying cash. He looked at me and said, "No problem." I left the meeting thinking, *Hmm, maybe he is for real after all?*

On Monday morning, I followed up with Mary, our in-house lender, and she said Jerry could buy as many properties as he wanted. I was a little surprised at this and decided I better get to work. Since I had no idea what I was doing, I asked Cody for help, and he turned me in the right direction. So Jerry and I started working together.

My new client always treated me like the expert, like I must know what I was doing; he would ask my opinions on properties and listen carefully to my responses. It wasn't long before I found a property he wanted to submit an offer on, and he asked me if I could bring the contract by his house so that his wife could sign it also. I agreed and later that day headed to his place. I had heard of the neighborhood he lived in but had never been there; it was a high-end part of town. As I turned into his driveway, I rechecked the address. The large gate slowly clanked open, and I drove in. I had never seen a house this nice, ever. I was instantly nervous. At the time, I was living in an apartment and driving a leased Jeep Cherokee. It was fairly new but not very impressive. I felt out of place and very intimidated.

Jerry greeted me at the door and invited me in. His home was beautiful and decorated with unique furniture that lent an Asian feel to it. Through enormous bay windows I saw a swimming pool in the back. As soon as we sat down at the dining room table, his wife walked in. She was stunning. Her name was Helena. She was Asian and looked like a movie star—thin, with lots of makeup and big hair. She stared at me and didn't say a word. Feeling self-conscious, I could tell she was deciding what my angle was with her husband. Women can always see through other women. Then she signed the contract without reading it. Jerry thanked me, and I left. I knew this was a turning point in my life; I could feel it.

Chapter 9
A Clue

After some restless sleep I awoke early on Sunday. Per custom I made a coffee and took it out to my favorite chair on the deck. I stared at the ocean and tried to clear my head as the same question drifted across it repeatedly. *Who is this guy?* I just had to find out.

My first call was to Sandy. Maybe Blake was a friend of hers; after all, he'd been to her house twice in the last week. I dialed the number and Sandy cheerfully picked up with a "Hello!"

"Hi Sandy, this is Paulina. How are you?"

"Great! I'm getting ready to visit a friend. We're going up to wine country, leaving town tomorrow."

"Wow, that sounds like fun. I have a question regarding one of the guests at the open house yesterday. I'm wondering if you know him—Blake? He was at your happy hour party too."

Sandy quickly responded, "I don't know him, but I know of him. He's a friend of Thomas Weaver, who was a previous owner of your house. Then years ago, another couple bought it from him. Blake lived with Thomas for a while before Thomas sold the place. Thomas was a kind man, but rumor was his wife had an affair with a younger man. I don't know much about Blake, other than he sure is a cutie. If I were a few years younger, who knows what could happen." She laughed loudly.

"I see." I paused and thought about the name Thomas Weaver. *I know that name… Wait, I know who that is!* I broke from my thoughts, gave a laugh in return, and said, "Okay, I was just curious. Have a great trip! I'll send you an update tomorrow." I hung up thinking, *Blake lived with Thomas Weaver in my house?! That's so weird. I need to find out more about this guy.*

Aside from my workout, I relaxed for the whole day. I was exhausted from the open house and was feeling agitated and anxious, as though I were waiting for something to happen. Anxiety was rampant in my family; my mom, sister, and brother all took anti-depressant medications. Not surprising, based on our past, but I refused to accept any drugs and have always been able to keep it under control.

Monday morning, I was determined to get back on my game. I started by reviewing the list that my guests signed upon visiting the open house—and realized Blake had not signed. *Well, this is just great. Now I don't even know his last name!* As I reviewed the record further,

I concluded there were no real prospects, except possibly the lady who had walked in and back out and identified herself as Chelsea. I should have asked her whether she was looking for herself or a client. Then again, I'd learned that buyers in this price range do not like questions. I typed up a quick summary for Sandy and emailed it over, adding optimistically that I was certain we would find the perfect buyer. But inside, I was freaking out. This listing was different. I needed to sell it, not only for the funds but for my image. A lot was riding on this one. I took a deep breath and said a prayer.

Chapter 10

The Bond

Jerry and I continued to look at properties together. I made him a priority and searched for more investments for him every day. He was indeed a real buyer; he soon closed on two properties, which led to a steady stream of income for me. I was so excited about my new life. I was closing six deals a month, working steadily, and making more money than I had ever seen before. I was also spending money fast. I bought a new Lexus, though I did have to take out a loan for it; I also bought new home furniture for me and for Patricia as well. It felt really good to be able to buy the things I wanted. I had never had money like this, and I was addicted. I became a workaholic.

Jerry was a kind man, and I could tell he liked me in a fatherly sort of way. He was quiet, but when he did speak, he had something interesting to say. One afternoon while we were out looking at properties, I asked him whether he had any children. He replied that he had a son named Riley, who was now twenty-one. Riley had been in a severe car accident at the age of sixteen. They'd expected him to die, but he pulled through. He had lasting health effects, however: one leg was amputated while the other was deformed, causing him to drag it as he walked. His speech had also been affected by his injuries. He had married a girl whom Jerry did not care for, named Samantha. Jerry said that she was out to take whatever she could from his son; he was sure that she did not love Riley and was only after his trust fund.

There was nothing he hated more, said Jerry, than people who tried to benefit from others without earning their own money honestly. He was a self-made man and did not respect the "takers" in the world. I agreed with this mind-set wholeheartedly; I knew I could marry an older man with money—I had the looks for it—but I could never be with someone whom I did not respect or to whom I was not attracted or in love with.

I felt sympathy for Jerry as he told me his son's story; he teared up and could barely get the words out. At the hospital immediately following the accident, he said, the emergency physician had told him and Helena to go and say goodbye to Riley. I myself was fighting back tears at Jerry's heartbreaking pain.

Over time I formed a bond with Jerry that I had never experienced before. I did not trust people, nor did I even like most, but my relationship with him felt different, in an unusually pleasant way. I knew for sure that God had sent Jerry into my life for a reason.

CHAPTER 11
WORDS MATTER

Later that week I worked on a marketing piece that would be mailed out to a select list of VIP buyers. I always designed my own marketing pieces; I knew that no one else could showcase a property better than I. It needed to be extremely detailed. I was intensely focused, so when my phone rang I wanted to silence it, but sighed and picked it up anyway. I didn't recognize the number—it was international.

"Paulina speaking."

"Hello, this is Chelsea McCarthy. I am representing Mr. Blake Parker. I would like to present an offer on your listing located at 1407 Tortoiseshell Drive. I want to inquire about the specifics of the property." Her voice was calm, cold, and very direct.

The name screamed in my mind. *Blake as in* the *Blake?!* I felt my heart race but was able to respond with a tranquil, "I see. How can I assist?"

"I want a list of the inclusions and exclusions and a timeline for possession. I would also like a list of any major renovations that have been completed on the property. How soon can you provide this information?"

If there was one thing I was good at, it was negotiating, and the first conversation sets the tone. It determines who is in control. As of that moment, Chelsea was in control. I paused, as I always found silence to be a useful negotiating tool, then stated, "May I ask you a few questions about your client?"

"Potentially, yes."

"Is your client securing financing for the purchase of the property?"

"No, Mr. Parker will be a cash buyer."

"I see. I will need proof of funds, and if you can provide that to me today, I can send an offer with your requested information by 10 a.m. tomorrow. Does that work for you?"

"Yes."

I paused again. "Great. Also, what is Mr. Parker's time frame for closing?"

"As soon as possible is preferred. We can close as soon as the title commitment and due diligence is complete, twenty-four days."

"Okay. I will await the proof of funds, and in the meantime, I will work on the information that you have requested. We do have a significant level of interest in the property. As you know, it is the most coveted property in Bel Air Estates. I will keep you apprised if another offer comes in."

Chelsea acknowledged this and ended with, "Good day."

I set the phone down. *This Blake has $20,000,000* in cash *to buy a house?* Now that I knew his last name, I could start my research on him. I took a deep breath and braced myself for what was to come.

CHAPTER 12
I WANT YOU

I continued to work around the clock at Remington Homes. One Friday afternoon, Cody and a few of the girls at the office invited me out to happy hour. Cody himself didn't drink, so he offered to drive all of us girls there and afterwards to our homes. I didn't get out much due to work, so I decided to go with.

As we chatted over our drinks, I glanced across the bar. There was an attractive man in a business suit alone and sipping whiskey. I liked the way he looked and the way he kept to himself. At that time I had not been with a man in several years; I did enjoy sex but found the complications of relationships to be too distracting to my life and not worth the trouble. But there was something different about this one that caught my eye. Our gazes met and he smiled slightly—kind of a half-smile, kind of a smirk. His hair was sandy brown and wavy, his eyes were light; they looked green from where I was sitting. I chatted with Cody, mostly about work-related things, as the other girls giggled and gossiped. After about an hour, the man got up and walked towards me. He was tall and lean; he walked with a purpose and had a confident air about him. He walked directly up to me, handed me his card, leaned in, and said, "I want you." I laughed a little and started to speak, but he turned and left without another word. I had to hand it to him; no one had ever approached me like that. I looked at his card. His name was Austin Hunter. He worked with Investment Portfolios at an address on Prospect Street, which was a very affluent area.

I was intrigued. The words "I want you" replayed in my mind.

CHAPTER 13

BITCOIN

I Googled "Blake Parker" and found a professional baseball player with that name, but it wasn't him. I checked some of my other go-to sites and couldn't find anything on him. Next I checked public records to see if he owned any real estate under this name, and nothing came up. It seemed as though Mr. Blake Parker was flying under the radar. If he had $20,000,000 in cash to buy this house, where did he get it from?

I started to prepare the information Chelsea had requested, just in case she did provide proof of funds. Though I tried to focus on a few other things, I couldn't help but keep checking my inbox for an email from Chelsea. At 6 p.m., I still had not heard from her. I went for a walk on the beach and decided that it most likely come to nothing. *Why do some people waste others' time?* I asked myself this question many times during my real estate career. I went back home and made a salad with fresh scallops for dinner, then poured a glass of Chardonnay and went out to the deck. By now it was nine, and I was about to go to bed early when I heard a *ping* from my cell phone.

I checked the notification. It was an email from Chelsea. I opened it to find a message from her.

See attached.

I opened the attachment. It was an account statement with the account number blacked out and Blake Parker's name at the top as the owner. I noticed right away it was not a typical bank statement, so I went into my office and printed it out. It was a statement showing $42,000,000 in Bitcoin. I was shocked. Bitcoin was relatively new and controversial as an acceptable form of currency, and I had a feeling Sandy would not be impressed that someone wanted to buy her home with it.

I held off on responding, since it was after business hours. If there was one thing I had learned, it was that if you respond immediately, any time of day or night, people will expect that availability from there on out. It is a matter of managing your time and your schedule. Some people think realtors are on call when in fact a successful realtor is not; they work business hours and take time off like any other professional. This is something I learned the hard way, being a recovered workaholic.

I went to bed wondering about Blake and how in the world he had gotten that much Bitcoin. The next morning, I awoke early feeling anxious. I decided to call Sandy and let her know about the potential buyer. She answered the phone with, "Hi, Paulina."

I decided to cut to the chase—I knew she was on vacation. "The young man that was at your happy hour and the open house, Mr.

Blake Parker, is interested in your property. His agent is suggesting they will make an offer. I requested proof of funds, and she sent over a statement showing $42,000,000 in Bitcoin." I paused and waited for a response.

Sandy said incredulously, "Bitcoin? Isn't that underground money that drug dealers use? I don't want any part of that! You can tell them I am not interested!"

Not surprised at her reaction, I replied, "I understand. I will find out more about his qualifications. I just wanted to keep you updated."

"Thank you, Paulina. What is this world coming to? I better run. Have a good day."

Without any more delay, I typed a response to Chelsea.

Thank you. The seller is requesting proof of funds in US currency.

Regards,

Paulina Paige

I received an immediate reply.

BITCOIN IS CURRENCY!

It's interesting when people communicate via writing in all caps. It seems as though they are yelling. Very unattractive. Clearly, I had hit a chord.

Chelsea,

I understand that Bitcoin is currency. However, its value can fluctuate, and the seller is not comfortable accepting this as proof of funds to purchase her property. She is requesting that Mr. Parker provide evidence of funds in US currency. I have the information you asked for and will send it to you as soon as the proof of the funds is provided.

Regards,

Paulina Paige

There was no immediate response.

CHAPTER 14

A MAYBE-DATE

I was loving my job with Remington Homes. There was a steady stream of business, and I admired my boss. Cody was sharp, witty, and the most charismatic person I had ever met.

I continued to work to find investment properties for Jerry. I was learning so much with each deal we closed, and I was also learning from Jerry, especially in the way he would handle negotiations. I was young and still new in the business, so not a very good negotiator yet. I would observe carefully how he handled such things. He never made me feel like I didn't know what I was doing, even though I think he could tell I wasn't very experienced. I was such a hard worker and searched for new properties every day for him, I never missed a new listing and would do in-depth research to determine if it would cash flow and if there was equity. Jerry could see how hard I was working, and he was impressed. By now, we had closed five properties and were still looking for five more. I looked forward to the days when I went out to show Jerry properties. We would talk about life. He was the kindest, smartest man I had ever met.

On a Saturday morning a few weeks after happy hour with Cody and the girls, I was cleaning and organizing my apartment when I spotted a business card lying tucked into the side of my purse. I pulled it out and read the name: Austin Hunter. I smiled. His name was unique and had a sexy sound to it. I Googled him and found his company website. He was the founder and CEO, and they provided funding for start-up businesses and also invested people's money. It appeared to be a high-end company located in a very exclusive area. There was a photo of him on the website, and I felt a flutter in my stomach when I looked at it; he was even better looking then I remembered. What I recalled quite accurately was the buzz I felt when he walked over and gave me his card. I tried to find out more online about him. The website's "About Me" talked about his education and experience, but nothing about a family or hobbies. I was able to find his age, though—39. I filed the card away but could not stop thinking about him.

Later in the evening, after a couple of glasses of wine, I decided to call him. I had no idea what I was going to say; it was very spontaneous. I actually didn't even expect him to answer, since it was after hours and this was probably his business phone number. But he did.

"Good evening." He had a gentle voice. Not too loud, just the right tone.

I was so surprised that I almost hung up. Instead I said, "Good evening," and then, oddly, gave a laugh. He paused for a moment, and then he laughed also. He had a nice laugh, I liked it very much. A person's laugh always reveals so much about them. Then I said, "This is Paulina. I met you not long ago at Jing's. You gave me your card."

"Yes, I did," he said, and then he paused. "I also told you that I want you, and I do."

"Well, I'm not sure what you mean by that," and I laughed again nervously.

He chuckled again also. "I would love to explain it to you over dinner. May I cook for you at my home tomorrow night?"

I immediately said, "Well, I don't think so, I don't normally go to strangers' homes for dinner to find out how they want me."

Once more he laughed, in the same relaxed, fun, and easy-going way. "Well, Paulina, what do I need to do to get to know you well enough that you will come over, so I can cook you dinner and tell you more?"

"I'm not sure."

Austin quickly responded, "Would you feel comfortable going out on my yacht tomorrow for a cocktail? We can keep it short and not get into all the details just yet."

I replied, "I think so."

"Great, then I *think* it's a date." he replied. "Can I call you in the morning and we can firm up our possible date?"

"Sure," I replied with another laugh.

"Have a lovely evening, beautiful," he said, smiling through the phone, and hung up.

I felt giddy as a teenager. I was so excited to meet him. *His yacht? Does he mean a boat? What am I getting myself into?*

CHAPTER 15
A GOODBYE

Jerry closed on all ten of his investment properties. As my business with him came to a close, I realized that he was really the one who had given me a start in real estate. He had taught me so much and was so patient with me. He was not only the best client I had ever had, but my friend as well. He had such a gentle way of sharing stories, and I always learned from him. We had many good conversations about life.

After closing on the tenth property, I walked with him outside. I said, "I have something for you." We walked over to my car, and I handed him a gift basket I had made for him. It contained a bottle of champagne, chocolates, and a couple of candles. On the card, I wrote *Congratulations! I enjoyed working with you! Paulina.* I hadn't known what else would be appropriate to give him. What do you give a man who has everything?

He smiled warmly and said, "Thank you."

"Tell Helena I said hi. Let's keep in touch."

He turned and walked away. I thought to myself, *I hope I see him again—what a nice man.*

Chapter 16
Finally, Proof

Two days passed with no response. I checked my inbox nearly every ten minutes to see if Chelsea had written back.

Eventually I decided that Blake Parker must be a phony. He was probably involved in illegal activity, and that was how he got all the Bitcoin—who knew if it was even his. I would just continue to work on my marketing plan. Later in the evening, I was outside on the deck when I heard a message come through on my phone; I walked into my office, there was an email from Chelsea.

See attached.

It was a statement from a bank in Switzerland showing US$32,000,000 in funds. It was in the name of a corporation, Parker LLC.

I decided to wait until the morning to respond.

Chelsea,

Thank you. Please provide documentation that Mr. Parker is the owner of this corporation.

Regards,

Paulina Paige

There was no immediate response from Chelsea. The next morning at seven I received an email with another attachment from her. The only message, all in caps again, was:

CONFIDENTIAL

Attached was a registration form for a corporation named Parker LLC, based in Switzerland. It looked legit, so I responded positively.

Thank you. Please see attached requested information. I attached the info Chelsea requested.

Regards,

Paulina Paige

Now it was up to Chelsea to present a written offer. Blake would need to provide one million dollars in earnest money with the contract. The ball was in their court.

The next morning, I was making my coffee and still waking up when my cell phone rang. I didn't recognize the number but answered anyway. "Hello, Paulina speaking."

"Hello, Paulina," said a man. I didn't recognize the voice until— "It's Blake Parker."

I paused and replied, "How are you?"

"I'm well, thank you. I understand that you have been in touch with Chelsea regarding an offer on your listing?"

"Yes, that is correct."

"I want to confirm that she has provided you with all of the financial information to your satisfaction?"

"Yes, I believe that she has. Upon receipt of a formal written offer I will submit it to the seller."

"Wonderful. I want to schedule a time to view the property in more detail. The view from the deck was exquisite, and I would like to see the rest."

"Yes, of course. When would you like to see it?"

"I am available anytime that works for you. How about tomorrow at noon?"

"Perfect. I will confirm with the seller and get back to you. Is this the best number to reach you?"

"Yes, it is. I will be back in touch. Have a lovely morning, Paulina." He hung up.

What is going on?! He sounded so professional, as though the incident on the deck never happened... Strange indeed!

I immediately called Sandy, who was still out of town, and she approved the showing, though she warned, "Be careful with him, he may be a criminal. I don't trust those Bitcoin people. I can have my security guard stop by if you would like?"

I told her I would be fine but thanked her all the same and told her I would call her after the showing with feedback. Now, I had to prepare for the next day. What to wear?

CHAPTER 17
ON THE YACHT

I awoke early on Sunday, feeling nervous and excited about the prospect of meeting Austin. The intrigue was at an all-time high and I couldn't wait to see what his next move was.

I was still working a lot of hours at Remington Homes and rising to the top among my colleagues. I needed to work less, but so far, I had no clear reason to cut back. On Sunday morning I was working in my home office preparing for the coming week when my phone rang. It was Austin; I had added him to my contacts. Biting my nails, I answered on the third ring. "Hello?" I said, like I didn't know who it was.

"Good morning, darling. This is Austin. I'm calling to see if our 'maybe' date is on for tonight?"

I smiled and giggled. I couldn't believe how much I loved his voice. I replied, "I think so."

"Well then, I think so too! How does a sunset cruise sound? You can meet me at the dock at four, and we will sail away?"

"Well, I *think* that sounds good," I replied. My voice sounded strange, as though I could not decide on anything to save my life.

He laughed and said, "I can't wait to see you."

When we hung up, I started to panic. *What in the world can I wear on a boat?* It had to be casual but still cute. I don't dress casually well. I started looking in my closet. I hadn't been this nervous for a date—or been on a date, period—in a very long time. I decided on a white cotton skirt and black tank top, and I grabbed a lightweight black and white sweater to take along. I added flat sandals and some new diamond earrings and wore my hair down, lightly curled.

Later that day, I drove to the dock and parked. As I walked up to the pier, I realized I didn't know what kind of boat he had; they all looked similar, and there were many. I stopped and watched as a giant yacht approached, and the next second I recognized Austin as the captain. He had a massive smile on his face.

"Welcome aboard."

I climbed up, grateful I'd worn my flat sandals. Giving me a hand, he said, "I'm glad you came. I have been looking forward to seeing you all day."

As we made our way out into the bay, Austin set the sails on coast, so he wouldn't have to drive. It was a beautiful evening, and the sun was just starting to set. He pulled out a bottle of champagne, popped the cork, and poured into two tall crystal flutes. Handing one to me, he sat back in his seat to look at me. I thought I might be blushing; I quickly started talking to break the silence.

"Do you come out here often?" I took a sip quickly, thinking, *What a stupid thing to say.*

He smiled. "Not as much as I would like, I would love to be out here every day around this time, and I would like to be here with you."

He is so direct, and he just met me!

Then he turned on some music and brought out appetizers. I was impressed by the food he had prepared—I could tell it was all homemade. Lobster rolls, crab cakes, fresh salad, and a delicious key lime pie. We finished the champagne and the food, and then he opened another bottle. I was feeling good and having one of the best times I have ever had in my life. We were chatting about life and silly things; there was no mention of questions like, *What do you do? Where do you live? Have you ever been married?* I didn't care, and I didn't want to change the vibe we had in the moment.

As it was starting to get dark, Austin turned the yacht around and started slowly back toward the dock. He looked at me and said, "You asked me what I meant when I said I wanted you."

"Yes, I did," I replied with a laugh.

He looked in my eyes and said slowly and genuinely, "I want to see you smile, I want to see you laugh, relax, sleep, make love... I want to please you in a way that no one else ever has or ever will. I want to start by cooking you dinner at my house this Friday evening. Are you interested?"

All I could say was, "Yes, I am."

"Great, I got a definite yes this time. Cheers!"

As we approached the dock, Austin leaned over. He kissed me on the neck several times, slowly working his way up to my lips. He paused and then kissed me so passionately I could barely breathe. When it was over I whispered, "Thank you, I had fun," and stepped out. I was relieved to get back into my car to regroup. This man was intense, and I had a feeling I was in deep.

CHAPTER 18
A BIG OPPORTUNITY

It had been over five and a half years now I'd been with Remington Homes. I became exponentially more confident in my real estate deals, and Cody offered me a higher commission split so as not to lose me to another company. I'd been living in the same old apartment for forever, and it finally seemed like time to start looking for an upgrade. So I started scouting for a good deal on a condo in my price range. Life was good.

It had been five years since I sold Jerry the last investment property. I still thought about him occasionally and sent him a card during the holidays. I was driving home from an appointment when I saw his name show up on my phone. *Jerry's calling me!* I answered with a smile. "Hello, Jerry!"

"Hi, how are you?"

"I'm great. It's nice to hear from you!"

"Helena and I are thinking of purchasing a new house. We are going to let our son and daughter-in-law move into our home, since they're having a baby. We want to start looking soon. Are you available to assist us?"

"Of course! I would love to. Thank you for thinking of me!"

"Of course," he replied. "We have a home we would like to tour. I'll send you the address. If possible we would like to see it this weekend."

"Great! I'll schedule it." I hung up, was so excited to work with him again. *I wonder where they are looking?*

When I got home I changed clothes and went into my home office to see an email from Jerry.

Paulina, here is the address of the property we would like to view.

Thank you, Jerry

18 Village Rd.

La Jolla

Immediately I thought, *That sounds like a nice area. Where is it?* I couldn't log in fast enough to pull up the listing. When it popped up, my heart skipped a beat. It was located in Bel Air Estates, one of the most exclusive areas in La Jolla. I had never been there before; it was gated and on the oceanfront. I'd heard that some celebrities had homes there.

The list price for this particular house was $10 million. I could barely believe my eyes at this number. *I don't even know how to write $10 million.* I had never sold a home over $950,000, so I was seriously freaking out. All my insecurities rose back up: *I'm not smart enough, not educated enough, I won't be able to write the contract. They will all know I'm not qualified to do this.* A full-blown anxiety attack rattled through me. It took me a couple of hours to calm down. I went to bed but did not sleep.

In the morning I looked at the email and the listing again several times, and then forced myself to pick up the phone and call the listing broker. Her name was Edith Collins, and she was with a high-end real estate company. Remington Homes was a lower-end real estate company, and we both knew it.

"Edith Collins, how can I assist you?"

I started off with a stammer. "H—hello, this is Paulina Page and I would like to schedule a tour for your listing located on Village Road for this Saturday."

She paused. "What is the name of your company?"

I stuttered again, "Oh, Remington Homes."

This time, the response came quickly. "Ms. Paige, is your client qualified to purchase this home?"

"Yes," I replied, trying to sound confident.

"How do you know they are qualified?"

"I know them personally. They are long-time clients of mine."

"I see," she replied in a bitchy voice. "Can you send us a pre-approval letter before Saturday?"

I responded softly, "I don't think it will be a problem. I will call you back."

Edith ended with, "Fine. Goodbye."

I called Jerry right away and told him the listing broker was requesting a pre-approval letter. He said he would be getting a small loan and was meeting with his mortgage lender that afternoon; he could send the letter over to me afterwards. Next he asked me if I had any thoughts on the area and whether the home was priced correctly—typical of Jerry to ask me advice on something I knew nothing about. All this was so over my head, it was crazy. I responded the way I always did with him: "I will do some research and let you know when we meet on Saturday."

"Wonderful!"

I closed my eyes and said a prayer: *Dear God, thank you for this opportunity. Please help me to do an excellent job for Jerry, to be confident and centered, and give me the wisdom to ask the right questions. If this is the house for them, let everything fall into place and to go smoothly. I am grateful for all that you have given me. I love you. I ask these things in the name of Jesus. Amen.*

I did not really consider myself a religious person, that is, I never went to church; but I was a big believer in God. Throughout my life, God had always been there and helped me through so many things. I remembered praying daily as a child for the safety for myself, my mother, brother, and sister, and always ending the prayer the same way: *Please get me out of here and into a better life.* I knew in my heart that God was there with me as a child, guiding me toward my future.

When I received the pre-approval letter from Jerry, I sent it straight to Edith. She confirmed our appointment to tour the home on the following Saturday at 1:00 p.m. My dinner date at Austin's was Friday night. I was feeling overwhelmed and excited for a big weekend.

CHAPTER 19
THE MOMENT THAT CHANGED EVERYTHING

My first thought upon waking was, *I have to show Blake the property today.* The idea of seeing him again made me nervous. His approach had been strange, and his proof of funds in a Swiss bank account and Bitcoin made me wonder where exactly he'd gotten his money.

After a spin class and a walk on the beach, the next step was deciding what to wear. I needed to look professional and not too sexy, but I wanted to look my best. After throwing almost everything out of my closet and onto my bed, I decided on a sleeveless white dress. It was form-fitting and probably a little too sexy, but I couldn't resist. I wore my new designer heels, which were the most expensive shoes I'd ever owned. I splurged on them after my last closing. The finishing touches were my sapphire-blue earrings and a matching bracelet for a pop of color. As noon approached, I was getting nervous about seeing Blake again; I needed to eat something but couldn't get anything down. My stomach was in knots. I wondered if he would bring

Chelsea with him. Usually, a buyer's representative would doubtless be present, but then again, nothing about this process had been normal.

I arrived at the house at 11:30 to allow myself time to turn all the lights, music, and waterfall. Fifteen minutes later I was ready and started pacing the way I always did when nervous. Then I saw Blake pulling up in the Cadillac he had driven to the party at Sandy's. *Why would a multi-millionaire drive that car?*

He looked better than ever in beige linen shorts, a black shirt, expensive loafers, and black Ray-Ban sunglasses. His hair was thick and wavy, parted to the side and cut longer in the back. He had a classy casual look about him that was hard not to appreciate. He parked and stepped out of his car as I peeked through the dining room window at him sneakily. He paused and spent several minutes just staring around at the house and the grounds. Then he headed towards the door.

I waited to hear the brass knocker before I opened up. Blake looked through me with those steel-blue eyes and smiled, saying, "Fancy meeting you here." He added a laugh and then walked in.

I tried to sound calm. "Welcome, Blake. Would you like a full tour?"

"What I would like is to see the view again. Can we go to the deck first?"

"Of course. The best view in La Jolla."

As we stepped out, we both naturally walked to the edge and took in the stunning view. Every time I stepped out onto that glass deck, it took my breath away.

We were both silent for a minute, and then I suggested, "Would you like to see the rest of the home now?"

"Sure."

We walked back into the house and I started my rehearsed tour. He watched me without saying one word. No questions, no comments—just watching me. It was very intimidating and made me uncomfortable. The sexual chemistry between us was intoxicating and hard to ignore, but I tried.

As we entered the game room, I began, "This is an amazing recreation room, perfect for entertaining."

He replied, "This would be a great place for a private party," from right behind me.

I felt him lift my hair up and slowly spin me around. He kissed me, and to my shock, I kissed him back. I was acting entirely out of character; I rarely dated and never even considered doing anything unprofessional at work. It was against everything I believed in. I'd worked too hard to get where I was to blow it by doing something stupid.

But he kissed me again, and again, and again. Things were moving so quickly, our breath accelerated, he was running his hands down my thighs and lifting my dress. He lightly touched me, and my body begged for more. Within a few seconds, he leaned me over the couch and we were having sex, right there in Sandy's game room. It was so passionate and erotic and unlike anything I'd ever experienced. As we rose to our feet, my mind raced. *I can't believe this just happened.*

I pulled myself together and stated, "I have to go. W—*we* have to go," I ended with a stutter.

Blake smiled and softly said, "I'll take it."

He walked out, and I locked the front door behind him. I was breathing hard and trying not to cry. *I am an idiot! Oh my god... What have I done?!* I quickly turned off all the lights and music, then locked up and drove home as fast as possible. My thoughts and emotions were jumbling and I kept berating myself over and over, *You're such an idiot!*

CHAPTER 20
SECOND DATE

I had a busy week at Remington Homes: I picked up three new clients and had a closing. Finally it was Friday afternoon and time for my second date with Austin. I was going to his place for dinner. I was excited and nervous, but also curious as to what his home would look like. I quickly Googled the address. It was in an upscale neighborhood a couple of blocks from the beach. I looked up the public record, and the title was in his name alone. He paid $1,500,000 for it three years ago, and now it was worth around $2,200,000. I was curious to learn more about this man.

I left work early so that I could get home and find something to wear. I'd wanted to go shopping that week for a new outfit, but I'd been too busy. I decided on a black skirt and a hot pink blouse with my black patent leather high heels. After one glass of wine, I Googled the address one more time. It was about thirty minutes from my apartment, and I knew there would be some traffic, so I headed out. As I got closer, I started to think more about Austin. I didn't know anything about him, really, except that he owned a financial company and a yacht and a house. I didn't know whether he had children or was divorced. I intended to find out more about him tonight.

As I pulled up, I noticed the landscaping was immaculate. *He must have a gardener to help him.* The neighborhood was beautiful; the lots were about an acre apart, allowing for privacy. I parked on the street in front of his house and took a deep breath.

I rang the doorbell, and a second later Austin opened the door wide with a big smile. "Come in, gorgeous! I am so glad you're here!" He was always so direct with his comments; it was refreshing.

"Hi there. You have a beautiful home!"

"Thank you. It looks better with you in it," he replied. He reached for me and kissed me. I was a little taken aback, but the kiss was beautiful—not too aggressive, just enough to feel our connection. He continued, "What can I get you to drink?"

"Do you have wine?"

"Oh yes indeed I do. Let's take a trip downstairs to the wine cellar. It happens to be one of my favorite places."

He led me downstairs to a stunning wine cellar. It was stone on the outside with an iron gate leading inward. Once inside, there was a separate tasting room which featured a table and two chairs and a loveseat. There were thousands of bottles of wine on the walls.

"Oh, my… I guess you do have wine," I commented with a laugh.

"Do you prefer red or white?"

"White would be great."

"Chardonnay? Can I introduce you to French white wine? If you like Chardonnay, I think you will enjoy it. If you don't like it, we have lots of Chardonnay too."

"Sure. I am easy," I replied.

"Easy, huh? Good to know." And he gave an attractive boyish grin.

The wine was delicious from the first sip. As we went back upstairs, I noticed the grounds in the back through large windows. There was a swimming pool and a hot tub and a beautifully landscaped yard. It was very private and tranquil. I was impressed; this was the most beautiful home I had ever visited.

Dinner was already underway. I could see that Austin knew his way around the kitchen. He had salmon on the plank ready to grill, a delicious pear salad, and wild rice.

"All of this looks so yummy!" I exclaimed.

He looked up from stirring the rice and said, "Yes, it does," with a wink, and I took another drink of wine. I had only dated two men in my life, and I'd never felt an attraction like this. It was almost like a fairy tale—the house, the wine, the food, and the man. I felt like I should say something.

"So, do you go to Jing's often?"

He looked up. "I would if I knew you're there. I was surprised to see such a beautiful woman at the bar. And I was curious as to who the man was that you were with."

"Oh, Cody. The owner of the real estate company where I'm employed."

"Real estate? Are you an agent?"

"Yes, I am."

"Excellent. I'm looking for the best realtor in the city to help me with a few real estate deals."

"Well, now you have connections," I replied and laughed. "And you are in the finance business?"

"Yes, I'm semi-retired. I love to spend time on the yacht, travel, and enjoy life. The first part of my life was all work and no play, and now I like to play. Does that sound good to you?"

I laughed again. "I'm in."

The wine was kicking in, so I made a mental note to switch to water after this glass. When the meal was ready, we ate outside and talked. I asked him whether he had any children and he responded in the negative, that he had never been married and was saving himself for the "right one." Then he asked me whether I had family in the area. I hated that question; family was the last thing I ever wanted to discuss. So I had a standard story I told: "My family lives in San Francisco, and my dad passed away a few years ago."

"I am so sorry."

"Thank you."

The conversation was lovely, and I was having a blast. After we finished our dinner, we went in and settled in the formal living room on the couch. In the midst of chatting, he reached over and gently kissed me. I was so attracted to him that my heart was racing.

He stood up, took my hand, and led me to the master bedroom, where the lights were low and the music played softly. He gently removed my blouse and skirt and his own clothes, and we made love. It was the best sex I'd ever had. I stayed the night and actually slept, which was highly unusual for me. Usually I could never sleep well unless I as alone in my bed. In the morning we had sex again, and he cooked a delicious breakfast—a vegetable omelet and fresh fruit. Afterwards I stood up and said, "I should go." He replied, "I had an amazing evening with you," and kissed me lightly, and I left.

As I got in my car, it occurred to me that he hadn't suggested getting together again. *What if this was just a one-night stand? What if he's a playboy that sleeps around?* The thought made me feel ill, so I headed home in a hurry.

But today was my showing with Jerry and Helena, and I had to be on my game.

Chapter 21
The Tour

Later that morning I was still feeling slightly hungover from the wine and slightly emotional and weird from the night with Austin. I had a bad feeling about the fact that he didn't say anything about another date. But for now, I had to set it aside and get ready for the most critical showing of my life.

I got a quick workout in to clear my head and then jumped in the shower. I decided on one of my most professional dresses, a solid navy blue dress with a high neck and a pearl necklace. Navy is the color for clear communication, after all; and since Helena would be there, I also wore my flat designer shoes. I looked at the listing again. I had prepared the comparable sales and the history of the property. A couple owned the property they purchased it ten years before they paid $6 million, and it now it was listed for $10 million. Prices had skyrocketed in the area, and the owners had performed a significant renovation on the property just last year. It seemed strange to me that they renovated it to that level only to sell it the next year. Overall, it seemed to be priced right; it was actually the lowest priced home in the neighborhood. I pulled up to the property and Jerry and Helena were right behind me. I was hoping to have a few minutes to reset, but my clients were present, so I had to be on my game.

I stepped out and quickly ran over to Jerry and gave him a big hug. I was so happy to see him. I smiled at Helena and hugged her as well. We stepped outside and looked at the home; it was beautiful and had striking curb appeal: stone and stucco ,with a tile roof. The exterior was painted deep forest green, complemented by stunning landscaping. A fountain ran next to the front door.

"I have some information for you that I will share after the showing," I mentioned as we walked toward the front door.

"Great," Jerry replied.

We knocked, and an older gentleman answered. "Hello. I was just on my way out, please come in. You can leave it unlocked when you are done—this is one of the safest places you can live." He was around sixty and attractive for his age. His eyes were green and his hair was brown with some gray in it, and he was fit. But he looked sad, and his eyes lacked spark.

"Thank you," I replied and handed him my business card, hoping he would not read it. I was insecure about working for Remington Homes when dealing with a house in this price range. He glanced at the card absentmindedly and left.

My clients walked into the kitchen, Helena to check out the appliances and Jerry immediately distracted by a glimpse of the view from the formal living room. He immediately stepped out onto the deck, and I followed. We both said "Wow" at the same time. The house sat up high on a bluff and overlooked the water with total privacy, no other residence in sight. There were more expensive homes in the neighborhood, but this had to be one of the very best lots. The hot tub was tucked away in the corner of the deck. Add to that, the indoor renovations were top of the line. The kitchen sported a contemporary feel with beautiful white Corian countertops and gray cabinets. The master bathroom had a new custom shower and a jetted soaking tub with custom imported tile. The basement was comprised of a fantastic theatre room, a game room, and an exercise room. I was utterly blown away; I had never seen a home like this, not even in magazines or movies. I tried to keep my cool, though, and not act like I was overly impressed.

We spent about an hour there. When we were finished and about to head out, Jerry reminded me, "Did you say you have some information for us?"

I opened my file and discussed my research with them. The comps showed that the property had been priced correctly. I shared with them, however, that I wasn't sure why they underwent such an extensive renovation project if they planned to sell so soon afterwards. Jerry thanked me and added, "I will review this tonight. Helena and I will talk about it and get back to you. Thank you for showing the house to us."

"You're welcome! It was great to see you!"

We walked out, and Jerry and Helena drove away. I was sitting in my car checking my messages when the man who had let us in drove up and walked over to my car. I rolled down the window.

"Do you have any questions about the property?"

"I don't believe so," I replied. "It is beautiful. The renovations are spectacular!"

He paused before nodding his head. "Yes, I thought we would be here forever… but things change." He looked down. I was silent for a few seconds, uncertain how to respond. He continued, "My wife had other plans." That's when it clicked. *Divorce. Now it makes sense.* I smiled as kindly as I could and said, "Thank you for allowing us to see it. Have a nice day."

I called Jerry to inform him about this interaction, then I went home and realized suddenly that I was exhausted. I changed into my nightgown and collapsed on the couch. I rechecked my messages, hoping I'd heard from Austin, but there was nothing. I had a sinking feeling that I might not hear from him ever again. I went to bed early and tried to forget about him, distracting myself with another prayer about the house in Bel Air Estates.

CHAPTER 22
FUTURE NEIGHBOR

I didn't sleep at all that night. I was completely horrified at my behavior at Sandy's house. That one stupid mistake could ruin my entire reputation. The thought had hit me—*What if Sandy had the cameras on? Oh my god! She might already know what happened!* Then I remembered I'd promised to call her after the showing. This situation was going from bad to worse.

I made some coffee and tried to calm down. The first thing I had to do was call Sandy. If she had the cameras on and knew what happened, I was definitely fired. *I* would certainly fire me. It was time to face the music and find out how bad it would be. I walked outside to the deck and sat down with my chin in my hands. My mind drifted to Jerry and I wondered, *What would he want me to do?* Strangely, after all this time I still thought of him as a parent figure—the kind I never had, the kind that always knew what to say and gave good advice. After some reflection I decided Jerry would want me to deal with this straight on and form a game plan for damage control. I had to move forward. Hiding would not help. So I went into my office and dialed Sandy's number.

"Hello Paulina, I'm glad you called! I was concerned when I didn't hear from you yesterday. I was going to call you, but I was at dinner with family and friends. How did it go with the undercover Bitcoin buyer?" she laughed.

I relaxed all my tensed muscles. *Sandy didn't know… at least, not yet.* Since she was out of town, she may not have watched the footage yet.

I replied, "I'm sorry I did not call yesterday! I had such a hectic day and the time got away from me. The showing went well and I did receive proof of funds from his agent. I'll send you a copy. I'm not sure if he will submit a formal offer, but it is a possibility. I'm continuing to work on the marketing plan and will keep you posted. If there is anything you need help with at your home while you are out of town, just let me know."

"Thank you, sweetie, you are so kind. I will be back this weekend. Talk to you soon. Goodbye."

I hung up and took a deep breath. That went better than expected, but I wasn't out of the woods yet. The next call I had to make was straight to the source.

Blake answered on the first ring. "Hello beautiful."

At his voice I paused and my heart skipped a beat. I decided to be direct. "I am calling to apologize for the incident that occurred at the property yesterday. It was inappropriate and should never have happened."

Blake quickly responded, "By 'the incident' do you mean when you gave me that lovely tour of the game room?" I remained quiet. "I enjoyed it very much and can't wait to revisit it again once I get settled."

"Settled"? Is he referring to buying the house? "Well," I replied aloud, "it was unprofessional and a mistake. I would appreciate it if you would keep it between us."

"Ah, a secret," he said. "I would love to have lots of secrets with just you. Since we're keeping secrets, how about if we *secretly* have dinner tonight?"

"No, thank you. I have to go, Blake, thank you for your time. Goodbye."

I felt flushed and slightly dizzy. Just hearing his voice made me feel like an insecure idiot. I would never forgive myself for what happened. I started to do some cleaning and laundry and tried to put it out of my mind. I always cleaned when I was nervous. So I paced and cleaned. I even turned on some music to drown out my thoughts. About an hour later, I heard a *ping* from my phone. I checked my inbox and read a new email from Chelsea.

Ms. Paige,

Attached is an offer to purchase the property located at 1407 Tortoiseshell Drive. I have already provided proof of funds as requested by you in a previous email. My client would like a quick response and a quick closing.

I look forward to your timely response.

Chelsea McCarthy

Exclusive Buyers Agent

I felt lightheaded, and my heart raced. I set down the Windex bottle and went into my office, sitting down at the desk. I pulled up the attached contract and hit *Print*. Then I brought it outside to the deck to review it. It was a full price offer: $20 million, all cash with no contingency. The earnest money was $1 million, as requested by the seller.

As I read through the contract, I had to admit it was well written. I was always very detailed with contracts and had learned that most brokers were not. I normally had to counter the offer to clean up the broker's mistakes. The only thing that looked questionable was on the list of inclusions—Blake asked for the furniture in the game room. Sandy did not offer to leave it, so I would have to check. Odd that he would ask for that; it made me uncomfortable to even think about that game room.

The closing date was twenty-four days from today. That was swift. I wasn't sure that Sandy could be out that soon. My next step was to meet with her and review the contract together.

I looked at the number again. $20 million. *It almost seems unreal. Can this be happening?* If this deal actually closed, it would be a game changer for me. All of my insecurities started to come up: *Am I smart enough to do this? Will I make a mistake on the contract?* And then, my next thought—*If Blake does buy this house, he'll be my neighbor... What in the world is happening?*

CHAPTER 23

LOWBALL

I was getting more irritated by the day. Forty-eight hours had passed since the hottest date of my life, and I hadn't heard one word from Austin. Clearly, he was a player. All that bullshit about "I want to please you and make you happy" was total bullshit, apparently. *Now I remember why I don't date or get involved in relationships. Such a waste of my energy and a distraction from my career.* I was mad at myself for falling for his smooth ways. Never married at thirty-nine should have been a red flag. So I decided to concentrate on my work and forget about him as thoroughly as possible.

I had not yet heard back from Jerry regarding the showing. I wasn't a pushy salesperson, but I decided to follow up.

"Hi Paulina."

"Hello Jerry, how are you?"

"Good, thanks."

"I just wanted to touch base and see if you had any additional questions regarding the property located on Village Road."

"Helena and I have been discussing it, and we think that it could be a fit for us. We want to submit an offer."

I was surprised by his eagerness. "Okay, what did you have in mind?"

"I would like to offer $8.9 million. I can close as soon as the seller would like. If it is a divorce situation, they may want a quick close."

I hesitated and thought about the offer. It was $1.1 million lower than list price. I was concerned that this was too low. The seller easily put $250,000 into renovations, and the comps supported the list price. I was surprised, as Jerry had never lowballed offers on the investment properties he had purchased. But after all, this was a whole different world. I was careful about what I said next: "Okay, I will start working on preparing the offer. They will most likely counter the price."

Jerry replied, "Well, let's see."

My next call had to be to the listing broker, Edith. I needed to know whether there were any other offers in or on their way in, so I'd know if we were competing.

"Edith speaking, how can I assist you?"

"Hello Edith, this is Paulina Paige with Remington Homes. I have a couple of questions for you regarding your listing on Village Road."

"Yes?"

"I showed the property last Saturday. I sent you my client's pre-approval letter, did you receive it?"

"My assistant will have handled that."

"My clients have some interest in the property. Do you currently have any offers on the table?"

"No," she replied, "but we have significant interest."

"What is the preferred time frame for a closing date for the seller?"

"They would like to close within thirty days."

"Is there anything else I should know about the property?"

"The seller will leave all the furniture if the buyer is interested."

Really? I was shocked. The furniture was beautiful and very high-end. "All of it?"

"Yes. Whatever they want."

"Do you mind if I ask why?"

"Yes, I do mind. Is there anything else, Ms. Paige?"

"No. Thank you. Goodbye."

Edith was bitchy. I have found that many people think that in order to be a good negotiator you have to be combative. Generally speaking, in a negotiation one person must win, and one must lose; but I believe that the best outcome is a win-win, when both parties feel like they were treated fairly and ended up satisfied enough. I Googled Edith to get a visual of her: she was around fifty, brunette, with straight hair styled in a shoulder-length bob. She dressed very conservatively and did not crack a smile in public. I had seen this type before; they were afraid to look sexy or fun, and believed they had to act this stodgy way in order to be successful. They were not very feminine or attractive. I did not ever want to turn into one of those realtors.

I called Jerry to inform him about the furniture, and he told me to include it the offer, as they were leaving most of theirs to Riley and Samantha. So I went to work on the proposal. When I finished it, I sent it to Jerry for signature, and he promptly signed it and sent it back. He never questioned me. I was nervous and kept retyping the number $8,900,000. I was afraid I would add or miss a zero in error. After reading the offer at least six times, I sent it to Edith with shaking fingers. I attached a cover letter.

Edith,

Please see the attached offer for the property located at 18 Village Rd. La Jolla. I have also attached a copy of my client's pre-approval letter. Please feel free to contact me with any questions.

I look forward to working with you.

Best regards,

Paulina Page

Remington Homes

One hour later, my phone rang. "Ms. Page?"

"Yes," I replied, knowing it was Edith on the line. She sounded even bitchier than before.

"I am in receipt of the offer you sent me on my very exclusive listing in Bel Air Estates. This offer is an insult! It is clear that this is not a price range you usually work and are not qualified to represent a buyer purchasing a home at this price point. I wouldn't even ask my seller to entertain an offer this level."

As she was speaking, I could feel my blood racing, and I was getting hot. *How dare this woman talk to me this way?!* When she paused for breath, I calmly said, "Edith, you are correct that this listing is on the higher end of homes I typically sell; however, I am certainly qualified and so is my client. You and I both know that you, as a listing broker, are required to present all offers. I expect a response from your seller by the acceptance deadline tomorrow at noon, per the contract. By the way, this is my client's highest and best offer." I hung up.

I was shocked by my own words. "Highest and best offer"? Where did I come up with that? I shouldn't have said it; it left no room for negotiation, and Jerry did not authorize it. I started to freak out. *Should I call her back? No, I can't.* I would lose all credibility, if I even had any in the first place. I had to leave it alone. So I prayed and waited.

CHAPTER 24
A COUNTERPROPOSAL

I reviewed the contract several times before I was ready to discuss it with Sandy. I couldn't believe this was actually happening. I took a deep breath and called her.

She answered on the second ring. "Hello Paulina, how are you?"

"Great, thank you. I am calling to let you know that you have received an offer on your home."

"Oh my! Is it from that Bitcoin boy?"

"It is," I answered. "I want to meet with you to review the contract. Are you available this afternoon?"

"Yes, I can make that work. I would like my son to be there, he understands all of that paperwork better than I do. Charles always handled all of that."

"That sounds good. I would love to meet him. Does four work for you and your son?"

"Yes. We will see you then at my house. Goodbye."

I arrived promptly at four bearing the contract and proof of funds. I knocked on the door, and an attractive young man around twenty-five appeared.

"Hello, you must be Paulina."

"Yes, and you are Sandy's son?"

"Yes, my name is Graham." He looked smart and sophisticated for his age.

Sandy came around the corner and smiled at me, saying, "Come on in, let's meet in the dining room."

I had printed out two copies, one for each of them and the original for me, and we started to go over the contract. Sandy was pleased that it was a full-price offer. "I think the price is a steal for this home," she commented. Sellers always think their home should be worth more than it is. I asked her if she thought twenty-four days would give her enough time to move out. She looked at Graham and said, "What do you think?"

"I think it would be fine as long as we know the deal is solid before we start moving your things. You can live with us and take the time you need to look for your next house."

I put in, "We could counter the due diligence deadline for ten days, which means that after ten days there will be no outs for the buyer. If he doesn't close he will lose his earnest money."

"$1 million, after the ten days, if all is a go you can start moving. How does that sound?"

"That sounds good," replied Sandy.

"Mr. Parker also wants to know if you will include the furniture in the game room?"

"That is odd," Graham commented.

"I don't mind," replied his mother. "It is older furniture, and I won't need it."

"Okay then… Regarding the proof of funds, he did provide this from a bank in Switzerland."

Graham looked at it and said, "Well as long as he has the funds at closing I don't think we care how he gets them."

I told them I would go back to the office to prepare the counterproposal and send it over for them to sign.

"Thank you, Paulina you sure do work hard!"

"Thank you, talk to you soon."

I did as I'd promised, and when Sandy had signed the counterproposal, I sent it to Chelsea without overthinking it.

I was out of my comfort zone on so many levels.

CHAPTER 25

PURE JOY

I was doing my best to not think about Austin, but I was constantly checking my phone. I couldn't believe that he wasn't reaching out to say anything at all after the most fantastic night together. He had to have felt something too. It was so strange. And frustrating.

I kept myself busier than ever at Remington Homes, Cody had been out of the office a lot lately, and rumors were circulating that he was selling the company to a large franchise. I was concerned and decided I would ask him directly next time I saw him. I'd had the option to move on to a larger, more prestigious firm for a while now, but I had stayed because of my loyalty to Cody. He taught me everything I knew.

The deadline for Jerry and Helena's offer was today at 5 p.m., and it was now 3:30. My stomach was in knots; I had not eaten anything all day. I wondered how Edith would handle the situation. I had a feeling she might send over a rejection notice and not counter the offer, especially since I'd told her it was the buyer's "highest and best offer." It was too late to keep second-guessing this; I had to let it go.

I was working on a contract for another client when I heard a *ping* on my phone—it was a text from Austin. *A text?* It had been six days with no communication at all, and now a *text?!* I opened it and quickly read: *Hi gorgeous, I hope you're having a great week. I can't stop thinking about you. Can I see you this Saturday evening?* My heart beat quickly and I was thrown off; he made it seem like nothing was wrong and the fact that I had not heard anything was normal. I was shaking a little, unsure what to think or do. I decided to leave it alone for now. I went back to work and tried not to think about the guy.

It was a quarter to five when another *ping* came through my phone. Feeling nauseous I opened an email from Edith with the subject line, *Re: Offer,* bracing myself for the rejection. There was an attachment, so I opened it immediately and saw the contract. I scrolled to the bottom, where the seller had signed it. Jerry was under contract on the house at 18 Village Road! I couldn't breathe. I screamed aloud, "Oh my god! Oh my god!" I jumped up and ran to Cody's office, but he was out of the office. I ran to the bathroom fighting back tears. *How did this happen?! No counter at all?*

$8.9 million, including the furniture! I was still freaking out in the ladies' room when my phone rang; it was Edith. I tried to sound calm when I picked up.

"Paulina speaking."

"Ms. Paige, this is Edith. I have sent you the executed contract. My client chose to accept your offer against my advice. It seems your timing was just right; he is ready to move on and liked the idea of a quick, no-hassle sale. I can assure you that if there are any hassles for my client throughout this transaction, the deal will crash. Do you understand?"

I paused strategically and replied, "I will send the contract to my client and arrange to have the earnest funds wired. I look forward to working with you and your client and to a successful closing. Goodbye."

I had to calm down before I called Jerry but was too excited to tell him the news. I dialed the number breathing hard and still shaking.

Jerry answered. "Hi Paulina—"

I blurted out, "They accepted the offer!"

He calmly said, "Excellent! You did a great job."

When he said those words, I felt the tears start to surface. I barely held it together. I thought about father's daily abuse during my childhood years and how no one had ever told me I did anything right, ever. He would say to me almost daily, *You're not worth anything, you're a dumbass. You'll never amount to anything.* Those were the words I heard every day until I was fourteen, and hearing these ones from Jerry somehow triggered something inside me and brought it back to my consciousness. I could barely speak. I was afraid he would know I was crying but I managed to say, "I will send you a copy and call you later."

I hung up the phone and, feeling overwhelmed with emotion, I sprinted from the building.

I drove home and cried harder than I had in years. Finally, exhausted, I forced myself to eat something. I had not eaten all day, and my face was stark white while my eyes were red and swollen. I was shocked at my physical reaction to this news. It was only 8:30, but I went to bed.

The next morning, I awoke around eight feeling groggy. I walked in the bathroom and was grimaced at my appearance. My eyes were swollen still, and were surrounded by dark circles. My skin was fair, so when I cried, it really showed. I rarely cried, though; it was like the floodgates opened yesterday. I was a train wreck. I was concerned about and taken aback by my state of mind and how fragile I seemed to be. Slowly, I made some coffee and went into my office. There was an email from Jerry.

Paulina, please advise where to send the earnest funds. Helena and I would like to go back to the property to measure some of the rooms and take a look at the furniture to determine what we want to keep. I would also like to schedule a home inspection for this weekend if that works for you and the seller. Thank you. Jerry.

This email hit me like a brick. I needed to snap out of it, so I gave myself a pep talk: *Paulina, this is your chance, don't fuck it up!* So I quickly responded.

Jerry, I have attached the wiring instructions you will need to wire $249,200 in earnest money to the title company. I will schedule the inspection and be back in touch. Congratulations! Paulina

I felt better already. Jerry had a way of doing that for me. I knew I'd feel even better if I went for a run, so I grabbed my headphones and started to jog through the nearby park. When I got back, I was feeling a lot better and more like myself. Running always helped me to clear my head; the wind on my face with the ocean over my shoulder calmed my soul. On my way to the shower I heard a *ping* on my phone and noticed it was a text from Austin. I realized I never responded yesterday—I was such a mess that I forgot all about it.

Hi darling, I am craving you. How about if we go to my beach house for the weekend? I hope you say yes. There was a winky face at the end. I read the text and thought, *He is so hot… and probably not good for me.* I wanted to say yes, but then I remembered I needed to schedule the inspection for Jerry on Saturday. I waited a few minutes and responded, *Hi Austin, that sounds nice, but have to work on Saturday, but I can find some time on Friday evening if that works for you?* He quickly replied, *Yes, of course, Friday it is. I can't wait to see you! Kisses.*

CHAPTER 26

A SEASIDE MEETING

I tried not to think about what was at stake with the offer on Sandy's house. Financially, it would be the break she needed to feel secure for the rest of her life. It seemed as though she must not have had the security cameras on the day of the "incident" with me and Blake, else she surely would have said something by now. There had been no contact from Blake, only from his agent. *Thank God.*

I tried not to dwell on the deadline for Blake to sign the counterproposal. Overall my amendment was a minor one, only adjusting the due diligence date to ten days. Chelsea had written the offer well, so there was nothing for me to clean up. The deadline was tonight at five, and it was now two. I decided to go for a walk on the beach. I had my headphones on and was enjoying the view when suddenly out of nowhere Blake was beside me. He must have run up from behind me. I jumped and screamed in shock, and he just laughed and lightly touched my arm.

"Hello beautiful! I didn't mean to startle you."

"Hi," I stuttered slightly and looked away.

He looked casual in a pair of swim trunks and a T-shirt. He was barefoot, and his hair was damp, as if he had been in the water. I tried not to meet those piercing blue eyes as he looked at me and said, "I am so excited to revisit the game room with you." He had that half smirk on his face.

I quickly replied, "Blake, as I mentioned before, what happened was a mistake. It should never have happened."

"Well, it certainly *felt* like it should have happened and like it should happen again."

"No, it will not happen again. I have to go."

Blake smiled and said, "We shall see about that. I will see you at the closing."

He was so arrogant that the appeal was starting to fade. I was disgusted with myself for what I'd done, and now all I wanted was to pretend it had never happened. I headed home cringing at Blake's closing comment.

CHAPTER 27

THE SHIFT

I stayed busy all week but found time to go shopping for a new dress. The coming weekend was important; I had a date with Austin on Friday and the home inspection for Jerry on Saturday. Austin hadn't specified what he wanted to do together, but I had a pretty good idea.

On Thursday I was at the office when Cody walked in. I hadn't seen him all week, and he looked rushed and stressed. I smiled and said, "Hi stranger, how's it going?"

"Fine, thanks," he replied and kept walking towards his office. He seemed distant, so I followed and asked him if he had a minute to talk.

"Uh, sure."

I walked in his office and sat down in the large leather chair across from his desk. "Well, first of all, I have some huge news." He looked at me with eyebrows raised.

"I have 18 Village Road in Bel Air Estates under contract!"

"What?! In La Jolla?"

Yes, I smiled proudly. The inspection is on Saturday."

"Wow! Amazing, Paulina. It must be over $5 million?"

"$8,900,000 but who's counting?" I laughed. I didn't want to jinx anything, but I had to tell Cody. I had not told anyone else.

Very seriously, he said, "I am so proud of you. I have watched you work so hard year after year, and you deserve this more than anyone... There is something I need to tell you, Paulina. I am selling the company to Better Homes and Gardens. They have made me an offer I can't refuse. I will most likely retire or at least try to. I have not told anyone, so please keep it a secret."

I looked down and said, "I heard a rumor but was hoping it wasn't valid. Thank you for telling me. When is this going to happen?"

Cody looked away. "In sixty days."

My mind was racing. *I can get Jerry's house closed, and then make a move for another company. No point staying here if Cody's gone.* The truth was, I was ready for a larger, more prestigious firm, but Cody felt like family to me, so I was sad. I said, "Congratulations, keep me posted!" and left for the day.

I got home around five and decided to make a salad for dinner and eat it outside on the patio. I was still renting the same old apartment, though my lease was up and I was month to month. I had been looking around for a condo to purchase but hadn't found anything in my price range. If Jerry's deal closed, I could finally afford to buy a house. The thought brought tears to my eyes. *This one deal will change my whole life.*

Later that evening a text came in on my phone. It was from Austin. *Apparently this man doesn't talk on the phone, only texts.*

Hi darling, I have a couple of options for you for tomorrow evening. A) I can pick you up at your house and take you to my favorite restaurant on the water. B) You can come to my place around 7, and I will cook you a delicious dinner and hope that you never want to leave, or at least stay the night. C) Anything you choose. Let me know what sounds good. Can't wait to see you! I had to smile. This man was charming and knew all the moves. I considered the options. I don't want him to come to my apartment; I was embarrassed to compare it to his home. So I decided on the second option. If the evening was half as fun as last time, I was definitely in. I replied, *Hi Austin, Option B is perfect! Can I bring anything?* He replied, *Just you. So excited! Kisses.*

Whew, this guy is hot. I resolved to let myself have fun and not read more deeply into the situation. *Why does it have to be something serious? I don't need serious right now.* After all, I was just excited to have a new dress to wear. The rest of the night I spent thinking about Austin.

CHAPTER 28
REALITY

Just thinking about Blake gave me anxiety. The conversation on the beach was strange; I didn't like how he refused to accept that our indiscretion was not going to be repeated. I was certainly confident that it would not.

It was a bit after four, and the deadline for Blake to send the signed counteroffer was five o'clock. I hated waiting for people, especially when the outcome had such a significant effect on me. So I paced impatiently. At a quarter to five, the email came through from Chelsea.

See attached.

Blake had signed the counterproposal and we were under contract, closing in twenty-four days. My heart skipped a beat. *Oh my god! Can this be real? Is this guy really buying the house?* The same thought as before came rushing in—*He'll be my neighbor!* I knew honestly that I really didn't like that, though I did like the idea of the closing. A check of this size would mean the break I needed.

When I called Sandy and told her we were under contract, she laughed and responded, "Oh my, I better start packing."

I should have been so excited, but for some reason, I felt uneasy. The thought of seeing Blake even once more made me feel nauseous. I would keep my distance and get through this. *Who knows if he will even close!*

I knew that there was nothing I could do to control the situation anymore; I had to let go or lose my mind.

The next morning, I received confirmation from the title company that the earnest funds had arrived. There was a receipt for $1 million. I had to sit down and process what just happened. Blake was serious, else he would not have wired the funds. I suddenly felt ill. The more the reality sank in, the sicker I felt at having him live so close. I found myself wishing I could change everything that had happened since I met Sandy, but it is too late. He was under contract and might very well be my neighbor in a few short weeks.

Chapter 29
The Hot Tub Date

Friday morning ushered in a busy day, but for the first time ever, I didn't want to work. I didn't even want to prepare for the home inspection with Jerry the following day. I just wanted to see Austin. After managing to make myself stay at the office for a few hours, I escaped home and started getting ready for the date. Things felt strained at the office these days, and a couple of people had already quit and gone to another firm. Cody was the glue that kept us all there, and due to the rumor of him leaving, things were changing quickly. I was trying to hang in there until my closing with Jerry was final. I would start looking at other firms the next week, but for now, I had other things on my mind.

I went for a run and then took a shower. I spent extra time on my hair and makeup and then put on my new black dress, which was tight-fitting and showed off my curves perfectly, hemmed above my knee. I slipped on my favorite heels and headed over to Austin's. I sat in my car for a few minutes before pulling up in front of his house; I was so nervous, I felt like a teenager. When I finally was calm enough to ring the doorbell, Austin answered quickly.

He looked incredibly hot. He was wearing a pair of jeans that fit just right and a white shirt and belt, and he was barefoot. With a big smile on his face he greeted me, "Hello darling, I'm so glad you're here! Come in."

I walked in, and he reached for me, wrapped his hands around my waist, and lightly kissed me. He paused and then kissed me again, this time whispering, "I can't stop thinking about you."

"Me too." I was breathless.

Then he led me into the kitchen and started kissing me more. His hands were sliding up my dress, and he was kissing my neck. It was so intense. Shaking his head he stopped and said, "I'll try to control myself, but I have to tell you that you have such a way with me. What would you like to drink, beautiful?"

"Wine would be great."

"White?"

"Yes please."

He already had it chilling. As he poured, he suggested, "Would you like to go outside while dinner's in the oven?"

"Sure."

We stepped out to the beautifully landscaped yard and took seats next to the hot tub, making small talk and laughing. He offered me another glass of wine and went to get it, and when he returned I was standing admiring the yard. It was a well-manicured, private oasis. He wrapped his arms around my waist and gently lifted off my dress, leaving me standing in my panties, bra, and heels. He continued to kiss me and then removed my underwear. I took off his shirt, he took off his pants, and the next thing I knew we were in the hot tub and having the best sex of my life.

What is happening to me?! I had never felt a sexual connection like this before. It was like I couldn't control myself around this man. I thought about him all the time. *I am in so deep!*

After the hot tub, I went into the restroom and put my dress back on. My hair was slightly damp and my makeup not looking great, but I felt amazing.

Austin and I had dinner outside by candlelight. He had prepared a delicious fresh sea bass with asparagus and wild rice. I was starting to wonder if there was anything he couldn't do. As we chatted, I asked him again why he had never married.

"I just don't believe in settling in life. It seems as though a lot of people do just that and then spend the rest of their lives being miserable. I live every day to the fullest, as though it's my last. How about you?"

Personally, the thought of marriage was the most ridiculous thing in the world to me after living through my parents' dysfunctional relationship. I would never even consider it. Marriage and my family were not something I liked to share with people, and I was always very guarded with my response to any related questions. My simple reply was, "I'm selective and have not met anyone that meets my criteria."

"I see," Austin smiled. "I want to learn more about your criteria."

We talked for hours about life without getting too personal. He was so smart and witty and had a way of making me relax. When we went back inside, we sat on the couch in the great room and kissed. We touched without having sex for a long time, until I was so turned on that I couldn't anymore; and then we had sex on the couch and went up to the bedroom. I slept well and woke up in his arms happily.

But the sun was shining really brightly, and I jumped up in alarm. "What time is it?"

"It's around 8:00, is everything okay?"

"I have a big appointment for work today. I should get going soon."

"Can I cook you something for breakfast first? You have to eat."

"Sure."

We sat outside, since it was a beautiful morning. Austin served poached eggs, quiche, and fresh fruit. We both had two cups of coffee. I was enjoying myself and feeling happy. He looked at me and said, "I love being with you."

"I—I like it too," I stuttered. "I should go now. I have a home inspection for an important property this afternoon."

"Cool, where is it?"

"In Bel Air Estates."

"Wow, as in *the* Bel Air Estates?"

"Yes, that's the one."

"I have a client that lives there, and I have visited a couple of times. It's incredible."

"Yeah, I'm really excited and nervous about it."

Austin replied supportively, "There is no need to be nervous, you're a rock star! You can do anything you choose to do. I can see it in your eyes—you have a spark and a drive that not many have. I don't know where it came from, but you got it, darling."

I laughed nervously. "Well, thank you."

He walked me to the door and kissed me lightly. "Goodbye, beautiful," was all he said.

I said goodbye and walked to my car. I felt strange—once more, no mention of getting together again. I had to let it go and accept that this was probably going to be a very casual thing. Good sex and good wine, nothing more. I headed home to get ready for the inspection with Jerry.

Chapter 30

Home Inspection

I decided on a navy skirt, white blouse, and flats. Out of respect for Helena, I wanted to look professional and not sexy. I knew this was the most important day of my life, and I did not underestimate any detail.

I arrived at the inspection fifteen minutes early. I parked and studied the neighborhood; the houses on each side of number 18 were larger and truly stunning. This house, though, had a beautiful Tuscan-style exterior, sat high on a bluff, and boasted one of the most spectacular views in the neighborhood, or any neighborhood for that matter.

When Jerry and Helena pulled up, we walked in together. This time, the owner was not present. The interior of the house looked somehow different this time; it seemed more contemporary and brighter. In fact, the light was beautiful throughout the house. Once again I was drawn to the deck outside. The view was genuinely stunning.

The home inspector soon arrived and began his inspection, and Helena and I met in the kitchen and chatted to pass time. I asked her how her son was doing.

"He's pretty well. As you know, Samantha is pregnant, and they're moving into our current house really soon. We are so excited about the baby... We hope Samantha is not too controlling and will let us help raise our grandbaby. Riley's not able to do as much, with his health issues."

"I hope so also," I replied. "Such an exciting time! Congratulations becoming grandparents, by the way. "

We chatted about the house and the upcoming process of moving in. Helena stated that the place had excellent feng shui, which had been her chief reason for wanting to see it again. I knew she had outstanding judgment and taste. Over the years, she had grown to trust me and like me; she recognized that I was not interested in her husband and that I was a hard worker. Though she never had to work or be concerned about money after marrying Jerry, she came from a low-income family and respected a woman who worked and made her own way in the world.

The home inspector spent four hours inspecting the property and then sat down with us to discuss. He informed us that the property was in excellent condition, and not only cosmetically. All the significant systems were new within the past year: the roof, HVAC system, and electrical. There were only a few minor items to discuss.

He added that he would send the report later in the evening for all of us to review, then left.

Jerry and Helena spent another hour going through each room and taking photos of the furniture to determine whether they would be using it. There were some beautiful, unique pieces of furniture that I was surprised the owner would leave behind.

I noticed a safe in the lower level, tucked in a closet off the exercise room. A closer look revealed that it was a gun safe. Jerry was right behind me, so I turned and asked him whether he could use it or he preferred it be removed. I didn't want him to have to bother with getting rid of things himself. Jerry replied, "No, I'll use it."

I always found it interesting for people to keep guns in their homes. I was afraid of guns. I could never shake the childhood images from my head of my father ranting with one in his hand. I associated all guns with that helpless fright.

I was silent, consumed in these thoughts, when Jerry looked at me and said, "Having a gun can save your life. It is like insurance—hopefully you will never need to use it, but you need to be fully covered, just in case. They don't have to be scary, as long as you are in control. It can give you power that you may need."

It was just like Jerry read my mind. I quickly glanced away, feeling a few tears coming to my eyes. I smiled and said, "Yes, that makes perfect sense!" Then I turned and changed the subject to the home inspection. Jerry said he would read the report and be in touch.

Driving home, I realized I was exhausted. The night with Austin was amazing but also emotionally draining. I always seemed to leave him wondering whether I would ever hear from him again. I had a few crackers, some cheese, and a glass of pinot grigio and got ready for bed. One more phone check revealed no text from Austin. I fell asleep reliving our last night together and wishing he would have called.

CHAPTER 31
DUE DILIGENCE

I spent the next week trying not to think about the upcoming closing with Blake. Since the due diligence period was ten days, he had three days left to cancel. At this point, if he did not close, he would lose his $1 million. The stakes were high.

At 7:00 a.m. I was having my first cup of coffee on the deck. This was my favorite time of the day; it was quiet, and my phone was not ringing yet. I enjoyed the time to reflect on and plan my day. But to my surprise, I was interrupted by a call. It was Blake. I felt instantly ill but gathered myself. I knew that I needed to deal with this head-on. I picked up on the third ring.

"Paulina speaking."

"Hello Paulina, this is Blake Parker."

"Hello, how are you?"

"Excellent, thank you. I want to schedule a time to complete the home inspection on the property. My agent is out of town, so I am calling you directly."

"I understand. When would you like to schedule this inspection?"

"Would tomorrow at five work for you?"

I paused and thought, *For me? How strange.* Usually the buyer's agent would be present, not me, as I worked for the seller. But I knew Sandy would not want him in the home without an agent. *Well, I guess I'll have to be present, but five would be a bit late for the home inspector.*

"Can you make it three?"

"Yes, of course, if that works best for you."

"Okay. I will confirm with the seller and get back to you."

I hung up feeling nauseous. I did not want to see Blake, and this was getting weird. Why was his agent out of town when this considerable deal was pending?

I called Sandy to ask whether the time would be okay for the home inspection. "Yes," she replied, "Graham and I have been packing, but we can leave for a few hours."

"Great. Thank you." I hung up, still feeling uneasy.

I did not sleep at all for anxiety. I even considered asking a colleague from my office to go to the inspection for me, but I knew that would be a cop-out. I needed to do this.

I dressed very conservatively the next day, picking out a black skirt, a dark navy blouse, low heels, and simple pearl earrings. I showed up at 2:30 to make sure the lights, the waterfall, and music were all on. I wanted to present the property in the best possible light for the inspector. The house showed beautifully; even with some packing boxes in some of the rooms, the home was straight out of a magazine.

Blake pulled up promptly at three. In tan slacks, a black shirt, and camel leather loafers he looked handsome; but I was not attracted to him anymore. I only wanted to get this over with as soon as possible. I opened the door and said, "Hello, how are you?"

"Great, thank you. How are you today, Paulina?"

It was all so normal and proper… and bizarre. Blake walked in and started to walk through the house, saying he wanted to measure some of the rooms for his furniture. I told him that the brochure contained the measurements for each room, but he said he liked to take his own. Trying to maintain my composure, I stayed in the foyer while he measured the great room and the master bedroom suite.

When he came out he said, "I would like to go out on the deck, would you join me?"

I hesitated. "What time is your inspector showing up?"

He smiled. "I am the inspector."

This was absolutely not normal. "You're not having a home inspection completed?" I couldn't help but show my surprise.

"I am inspecting right now, and I like what I see," he replied with that devilish smirk.

I felt uncomfortable and wished I had not agreed to be here. After a pause, I said I would wait for him in the kitchen.

"Maybe you can assist me with the inspection?"

"No, I can't." I decided to be straight with him, since I was irritated. "Blake, your agent should be here to represent you during the inspection. I agreed since she was out of town, but I am feeling uncomfortable with this scenario. As you know, I represent the seller and cannot advise you on inspection items, nor am I a professional home inspector. Please feel free to look around, and I will wait here in the kitchen."

With another cocky smile Blake said, "I don't want you to feel uncomfortable. I would like you to feel at home here. Just relax, I need to take a few more measurements. I want you to feel at home here."

What an odd thing to say. I was starting to markedly dislike Blake Parker and wanted to get out of there pronto. Sitting on a stool in the kitchen, I checked my phone and pretended to be busy working. When Blake walked back in, he suggested, "Let's have a toast to celebrate my new home and your closing." He pulled a bottle of champagne out of his bag.

I quickly replied, "No, thank you."

To my exasperation, he proceeded to open it. *This guy seems unable to take no for an answer.* So I rose and walked to the door, stating that Sandy and her son were on their way back. "We have to go now."

Still standing in the kitchen with an open bottle of champagne, Blake was noticeably upset with me. In fact, he looked downright angry, as though he was about to snap. He set it down and then quickly gathered his composure. "Well then, we will have to wait until after closing to celebrate."

"Looking forward to it." I walked out of the house, stood on the porch, and said blandly, "Goodbye. Have a nice day." I waited for him to pass by, then quickly stepped back inside and locked the door.

Things felt different now; there'd been a bad vibe in there. I decided I didn't like Blake Parker at all. I was so disgusted with myself for the mistake I'd made with him. *I must've been crazy to have done that! At least I was able to get rid of him today without him trying to touch me.*

I would not be alone with him again, ever. The strangest thing was, I genuinely hoped he wouldn't go through with buying the house. I decidedly did not want him to be my neighbor, and as much as I wanted the money, I would gladly give it up if I could be rid of him. But unfortunately, it was not up to me. Blake had three days to cancel or close, his choice. The clock was ticking, and there was a lot at stake.

CHAPTER 32

OVER MY HEAD

I received the inspection report for the Village Road property. There were a few minor items and some maintenance items, but overall it was a very clean home inspection. I took a deep breath. *I think this might actually happen.* I got really emotional at the thought; this deal would be a game changer for me in so many ways.

Once he got a chance to look over it as well, Jerry called and said they had decided not to ask for any repairs. Helena believed in "playing fair," he explained, and considering the price and that the seller was leaving the furniture, they already had a good deal. They also didn't want to make it more difficult for the seller than necessary, since there was a divorce involved. Helena was big on karma and believed what comes around goes around.

I agreed with him that we'd gotten a fantastic deal on this home. It appeared as though we would be closing very soon.

After five days, there was no word from Austin, not even a quick text to say hello. I was irritable and tired of checking my phone all day.

I kept telling myself that our "thing" was casual, great sex, and nothing more; but it did not feel this way in my soul. I liked him more than anyone I had ever met. Ever. Not only physically, either; he was really smart, and I loved being in his presence. I could actually *sleep* with him. I had never really slept with any man before. The truth was, I was falling hard for him, and I was hoping he felt the same way. It seemed obvious that he didn't, however, else I would be hearing from him. I refused to contact him myself: I believed the man should pursue the woman. I was old-fashioned that way. So I decided to try and not think about him. *Why can't relationships ever be easy?*

I still didn't expect to ever fall genuinely in love. It was just too complicated.

I called Edith, hoping to get her voicemail so I didn't have to hear her condescending tone. Unfortunately, she answered on the first ring.

"Yes, Ms. Paige."

"Hello Edith, I wanted to let you know that the home inspection went quite well. My clients will not be asking for any repairs. The loan is underway, and all looks good for closing on time per the contract."

A long pause followed by, "Well, just so that you know we do have a backup offer that is full price, so any delays on your end and the contract will void and we will take the other offer. My client now understands they should have taken my advice and rejected your lowball offer."

"There will be no delays. Good day."

I hung up praying I'd spoken truth. We were not at the finish line yet. One delay from the lender, and we were out. I called Jerry with the update, to which he replied, "No problem, we are on time. We know this is meant to be our home, and thanks to you, we are getting a great deal. We are starting to pack and will be at the closing. Please schedule for 8 a.m. on the day of closing. Thank you, Paulina."

I hung up, so excited that I jumped up and down a few times and then paced quickly from one end of the room to the other. I wanted to celebrate, but… I did not have anyone to celebrate with. I was alone. *What a depressing thought.* All of a sudden, without thinking about it, I picked up the phone and dialed Austin's number.

He answered with a "Hello darling." I was shocked that he answered and even more shocked that I'd called him. This was completely out of character for me. I never called men, ever.

I paused for a second and said, "I just wanted to say hi…" I considered hanging up for a moment. I felt weird, like this call was already a big mistake.

"Well, hi. I'm so glad you called, are you free tonight? I would love to take you for a spin on the yacht. I miss you."

"You miss me?" *Well, you could have fooled me.* But I did want to celebrate, and for once I did not want to be alone. "Sure, I will meet you at the dock in an hour."

"Perfect, I can't wait. Kisses."

I put on some beige shorts and a black tank top. I looked casual, but cute. Lastly I threw on my flat sandals and headed to the pier to meet Austin. As I walked up to the dock I saw him staring down at something; he didn't see me yet. He looked so sexy I could hardly stand it. As I approached, he gave a huge smile and called to me, "You look stunning." I jumped on board and we sailed away.

Within minutes of setting out into the bay, he grabbed me and started kissing me. In an instant we were both very into it. Still in our seats at the front of the yacht, he gently lifted off my shirt and slid down my shorts, kissing my body slowly as he moved lower. He kissed me all over, then we made love on the deck chair. The sun was just setting, and it was not dark yet; anybody floating by would be able to see us. We didn't care. It was amazing, like we were the only people in the world. Afterward, we lay down on the deck to catch our breath. He looked at me and said, "I am so glad you called. This is precisely what the doctor ordered." We both laughed, and he urged, "So, let's have that toast!" Opening a bottle of French white wine, he asked, "What are we toasting to, beautiful?"

"My deal in Bel Air Estates looks like a go!"

He grabbed me again and hugged me hard. It was such a genuine hug that I felt it in my bones. I didn't think anyone had ever embraced me like that before. Then he looked in my eyes and said, "That is so awesome! You deserve it." He poured the wine and made a toast: "To your closing going smoothly and to you finding complete financial and emotional security, to all of your dreams coming true, even the ones you don't know about yet! Cheers!"

Wow, what a toast. He was so smart and sensitive, especially for a man. I had always thought women are more intelligent than men, but this one made me wonder. We finished off the wine and headed back to the pier.

"Would you like to come over, darling?"

"I can't, I have to get back home tonight. I left in a hurry, and I don't have anything I need with me."

"Thank you for coming. I love being with you."

I replied, "Me too," and walked to my car.

This man is driving me crazy! I am out of my comfort zone and like him way too much. I went to sleep thinking of Austin, but not without adding a prayer: *Dear God, Thank you so much for the opportunity you have given me with the house for Jerry. I know it is a gift from you and that I could never do any of this without you. Help me to do an excellent job for him and Helena and for this to be a beautiful home for them that will bring them much happiness. Please also help me with Austin, I turn the relationship over to you and ask that you show me how to handle it. You know I like him too much, and you know how bad I am at this, so help me figure it out. I ask these things from you in the name of Jesus Christ. Amen.*

CHAPTER 33
TICK-TOCK

I was counting the days until the due diligence date. Finally it was here: the date that Blake would have to cancel or lose $1 million. I was still secretly hoping he would withdraw his offer and I would never have to see him again.

I woke up early after a restless night's sleep and got ready for a run on the beach. I grabbed my headphones and headed out. There was a cool breeze in the air, and the wind lightly brushed my face. I looked out at the waves and thought of Jerry. It was strange how he still came to mind at random times; maybe I felt as though he were looking out for me. The longer I kept running, the better I was starting to feel. Finally, I stopped at my favorite spot on the sand and sat down to catch my breath.

In quick succession I heard someone came up behind me and felt a touch on my shoulder. The voice was unmistakable.

"You look so beautiful this morning."

Blake's touch sent a chill through my body. I immediately jumped up and said, "I have to go," and took off sprinting towards home. I was freaking out. Something had seriously shifted. Now, just the sight of him turned my stomach. I didn't know what to do; this was the buyer of my listing and my future neighbor, and I couldn't stand to be near him.

At home I tried to calm my nerves. As the day progressed, I prayed harder and harder that Chelsea would call and say he was canceling, but I did not hear anything. By 9 p.m., there was still no word. I walked out to my deck and stared at the water. I knew Blake Parker was going to close on the house on Tortoiseshell Drive and that he would be my neighbor. The thought of moving crossed my mind, but I knew this was not a real option. I would have to find a way to deal with this man. After all, I had brought all of this on myself. I was an idiot, and now I had to figure out how to live my life in his proximity. I had to be able to run on the beach, walk on my neighborhood streets, or go to the local supermarket without constant fear of running into him. I had really gotten myself into a mess this time.

I didn't sleep at all that night. The next morning I made a cup of coffee and could barely function. I was emotionally exhausted. Then my phone rang. It was Sandy.

"Good morning, Paulina. Just checking to see if I should schedule the movers?"

"Hi Sandy. Yes, it appears that all is in order. The buyer has passed the due diligence deadline."

"Great, then I will move forward. I am planning a party before I move out, just a little get-together. I hope you can make it!"

"Thank you, Sandy, I would love to!"

I had the most significant closing of my entire life in front of me, a closing that would secure my future and finally give me peace of mind, and I was dreading it. *I have to get over this!* I decided to take the rest of the day off and try to regroup. I took a spin class at home and then sat outside and read a book. I rarely did this, but I had to reset. Then I went to bed early, trying not to dwell on the fact that Blake Parker would be my neighbor in fourteen days.

CHAPTER 34

GAME CHANGER

I was so excited I could not stop smiling. All was final with the loan, and the closing on Jerry and Helena's house was in two days—8 a.m. on Friday. This would be my most significant closing to date and would enable me to buy my own home. It was almost like a dream.

I awoke at 5 a.m. on Friday. Edgy and hyper, I paced the length of my apartment and talked to myself the way I always did when worried. *Everything is in order. I can do this.* I told myself over and over: *I can do this.* I was decidedly not looking forward to seeing Edith; that woman rubbed me the wrong way. I picked out a blue dress that I had only worn once. It was more conservative then I typically dressed, cut just below the knee and featuring a half sleeve and shell neckline. Next I put on a pair of pearl and diamond earrings and my expensive heels and styled my hair smooth. I looked very professional. It was about thirty minutes before I needed to leave, so I made a cup of coffee and walked out on my small patio thinking about how far I had come in life.

Back when I was a hairstylist, I was so happy to have enough money to rent my own apartment. *Now I'm going to buy my own home.* I would have a mortgage, but I felt confident that I'd be able to make the monthly payments. I thought back to my childhood and thought about my sister, brother, and mother. All three continued to struggle financially. I was close with Patricia—we talked on the phone and saw each other regularly—but Paul and Mom had stuck together and gone their own way. I rarely spoke with them.

Suddenly I had a flashback to a childhood moment. I was around five years old, still too young for school, but I was in the truck one morning when my father drove my sister and brother to school. My mom was at work. We were riding in his old beat-up pickup when Patricia realized she forgot her lunch money and told our father. He slammed on the brakes and fell into a rage, screaming, "I don't have enough gas money to be driving back and forth all day! You're in trouble!" He turned the truck around and headed back home, and when we got there he proceeded to beat all of us with the belt. Patricia felt immense guilt. We were all crying, and I remember thinking, *Someday I'll make enough money for gas and lunch.* I was only a little kid, but I knew this would not be my life forever.

I felt the tears welling up in my eyes and quickly ran into the bathroom to splash cold water on my face. Strange that this memory surfaced today after being buried for so many years. But I was not about to let it ruin the occasion. I freshened up my lipstick and headed to the most significant closing of my life.

I arrived fifteen minutes early. I always allowed extra time for traffic so that I could arrive fifteen minutes early to every appointment. When I walked into the title company Jerry and Helena were already seated in reception, appearing relaxed and smiling. They wished me a good morning and I reciprocated the greeting. Then Edith walked in, easily recognizable because of my Google search. She was brunette with a straight bob, dressed in a suit and flat shoes. She looked frumpy and bitchy. She ignored us completely and approached the receptionist to state, "I am here for the closing at 18 Village Road."

"Yes, please come with me."

Edith walked with the receptionist into the closing room. When the latter returned alone, I walked up to her desk and said, "We are also here for the closing on Village Road."

"Please follow me."

We walked into the closing room, and Edith glanced up from her phone.

"Hello Edith, my name is Paulina Page. This is Jerry and Helena Newman."

Without acknowledging Helena or me, Edith's eyes settled on Jerry and she said, "Hello, Mr. Newman."

I felt my temper rising and warned myself to calm down. I sat down next to Helena and waited for the closer to come in. The seller was not there yet either. A few minutes later he appeared—the man I had met the first time I showed the house. He seemed frail and sad as he looked at all of us and said, "Hello." I stood up, shook his hand, and introduced him to Jerry and Helena.

"Nice to meet you. My name is Thomas Weaver."

After all the closing papers were signed, we sat waiting for the closer to make copies for each party present. Thomas had been very quiet through the process, but now he looked at Jerry and Helena and said, "I hope this house becomes your dream home. It was supposed to be mine. I worked my whole life to be able to retire there. But my wife had an affair with another man, a much younger man, and decided she wanted more than I could offer. Now I know that a house is not a home if you are with the wrong person, regardless of how beautiful it is. But this is a unique property and carries very good and powerful energy."

Edith looked positively horrified that her client shared all of this with us.

Helena looked at him and said gravely, "I know the home has incredible strength. I knew it the first time I drove up before even going inside. And when I did enter, I could feel the intention that you put into it. I was certain that it was a beautiful place we could make our home. Thank you for allowing us to be the ones to live in it. We will treasure it for all of our lives and never forget you."

It was a powerful moment, so real and so much more significant than any other real estate deal I had ever been involved in. It was not just about buying a house; it was about an extraordinary home belonging to the right people. I was moved and felt myself getting emotional. I remained quiet, as did Jerry.

As we were walking out, Jerry looked at Edith one last time and said, "In the future, please treat Paulina and my wife with respect. They both deserve it."

Edith looked shocked that he had called her out. She did not say a word.

I put my hand out to shake Thomas's hand, but he reached in and hugged me. "Take care," he said.

We all walked outside. Waiting in my car I had a gift for my clients; it was a piece of art I had had a local artist paint depicting the new house. It was watercolor and very colorful and pretty. Wrapped in shiny pink and white paper, I handed it to them and said, "I hope you like it. Thank you very much for allowing me to assist you in the purchase of your home. It is always a pleasure to work with you. Let's keep in touch."

They both said, "Thank you. Yes, let's keep in touch," and hugged me.

I got in my car and sat in the parking lot, not really believing what had just taken place. I slowly opened the file, where my check was on top in an envelope. I looked at the number. $267,000. I had never had anywhere near this amount of money in my life. I felt like it was a dream. I started to cry; it was like everything in my life had led up to this moment. It was reality-changing, and I knew it.

I drove home and realized I had not heard from Austin. Again. I was so tired of wondering whether this was going anywhere that I considered just ending it. *I am tired of this total bullshit! Is he my boyfriend? Is he just someone that I can enjoy the best sex I have ever had in my life with, or is he something more?* I was walking up to my door when I noticed something on my front step. I didn't like to have packages left there for fear someone would take them, and I had not ordered anything to be delivered, so I had no idea what it could be. It was a beautifully wrapped gift box, wrapped in delicate light blue paper. I went inside and quickly opened it to find a stunning diamond necklace shaped as a teardrop heart. There was a card too.

Paulina, Congratulations on your closing! This necklace reminds me of you: lovely, delicate, classy, and smart. You are an amazing, successful woman and deserve all the best things in this life. I want to celebrate with you this weekend. Kisses, Austin.

Wow, this man knew how to flatter a woman. I didn't remember telling him that my closing was today, but I must have. I was pretty sure no one had ever told me I was smart. The necklace was so beautiful that once I put it on, I didn't ever want to take it off. I poured myself a glass of wine and called him.

"Hi," is all I said.

"Hi, darling! How are you? How did it go?"

"It went great, I still can't believe it happened, and the seller is such a nice man... And thank you for the gift!"

"You like the necklace?"

"Yes, I love it. Thank you."

Austin went on, "We need to celebrate! When can I see you? How about tomorrow?"

I was exhausted—deliriously happy, but exhausted. "Tomorrow would be perfect."

"I can't wait. Goodnight, beautiful. Kisses."

I went to bed feeling like that day must have been a dream. I was completely beat but managed to say a quick prayer: *Dear God, thank you so much. I know that all of this is from you, and I am grateful. Amen.*

CHAPTER 35
TRAPPED

I never dwelled long on my childhood; in fact, it rarely crossed my mind. I knew it had some lasting effects on me, but who doesn't have some issues from their childhood? I mostly chose to pretend it never happened and had a set of lies I parroted to people when they asked about my family. It was much easier that way.

I heard the scream from outside. It was the kind of cry that hits you in the gut and makes you want to run in the opposite direction. I was around seven years old and we were living in an old run-down house on a farm. A friend of my father had allowed us to live there for free as long as we paid the electric bill and fixed anything that broke down. My mom was the breadwinner and the only one working by this point, as my father had become a full-blown alcoholic and could not hold a job. The house was in a very rural area, so my mom's drive to her factory job was one and a half hours each way: she would leave the house at the crack of dawn and not get home until after dark. This arrangement left us alone with my father for long periods of time. Looking back I had to wonder how she could leave us with him knowing how violent he was, but I guess she was so depleted that she didn't know what else to do. Most of the days he would leave us alone and drink himself into oblivion, but after a few months of living there, he took a darker turn. It's almost like he was possessed—with mounting anger he would rant and rave every day, looking and acting crazy. I remember thinking that he was a monster. He became more and more violent against my mom, and the violence against her was always the scariest to me. If he killed her, we would be stuck with him forever. I dreamed of the day when I would never have to see him again.

It was an early Saturday morning when I heard the scream of terror from my mom. I ran into the kitchen from outside to see him holding a knife at her throat. He had that evil crazed look in his eye. I screamed, and he looked at me and laughed. I begged him to put it down, sobbing hysterically to the point of not being able to breathe. He dropped the knife, pushed my mom to the floor, crying, and walked out of the room. I rushed to her side and begged her to leave him like I had done many times before; I told her we could find a way, we just had to get out of there. To my shock she agreed.

I talked to my siblings, and we came up with a plan to escape. The next morning, Mom was in the car with the engine running, as if about to leave for work. Once we made sure that my father was in his bedroom, it seemed like a good time to go for it. I went first and dashed out the side door of the house and quickly made it to the car. Paul came next and dived promptly into the backseat. We waited for Patricia. She stumbled through the doorway with an expression of terror, and right behind her was our father. With one glance he knew what was going on. He lifted his foot and kicked Patricia with all his strength in his cowboy boots that were pointed and sharp in the toe. As she fell to the ground screaming in pain, we all knew our plan had failed. I jumped out of the car to help my sister. My father proceeded to brutally beat all of us, and we all knew we would never get away from him; this had been our one chance. Patricia felt responsible that she did not make it to the car, and I knew it haunted her for the rest of her life.

A few years passed and we moved to a different house in a more typical neighborhood. Of course, we were far from typical. We tried to fit in with the other kids the best we could, but we had to hide a lot from them. Mom had a decent job at the factory and made enough to support us. My father didn't work and continued to have outbursts, so there was always abuse as we were grew older.

Even before Patricia and I moved out, the three of us kids were choosing how we were going to live our adult lives. This was where I set myself apart from my brother and sister: I had no idea how, but I knew that I would find a better future. I knew there was so much more out there, and I was going to find it.

CHAPTER 36
THE CLOSING

I avoided the beach and stayed indoors to avoid Blake. The closing was coming right up, and I had not heard anything from him or his agent. But I needed to go to Sandy's goodbye party; it was essential to make an appearance for her sake, not to mention it was an opportunity for more business. I prayed Blake wouldn't show.

The night of the party, I put on my pink floral wrap dress and white sandals. She'd said it would be casual and, since the house was a mess of boxes, the party would be outside by the pool. I figured my outfit was perfect for the vibe. I sighed into the mirror; I was not in the party mood at all, and planned to stay only long enough to say hi to my neighbors. The party was from six to nine, and I showed up at 6:30 and found a parking spot close to the house.

I walked in with a bottle of champagne for Sandy, and she hugged me and said, "Thank you for everything, you are such a dear." I smiled and reciprocated. "Thank you, I am going to miss you." We both talked about keeping in touch but knew that it would not happen.

I went to the bar and ordered a glass of Chardonnay. I was mingling with a few neighbors when I spotted Blake. *He's here!* He was with Sandy, and they seemed to be in a deep conversation. Sandy looked serious. My heart sank. *What if he tells her about the... incident?* I started to sweat but quickly walked over to join the two.

"Hello, Mr. Parker," I began.

He smiled that cocky smile and said, "Hello Paulina, you look lovely this evening."

I felt flushed and was freaking out on the inside, so I glanced at Sandy to try and read the situation. She just looked at Blake and said, "So are you moving in this weekend?"

Blake grinned and said, "No, not yet. I have some shopping to do first. I am happy that you are leaving the furniture in the recreation room... Paulina was kind enough to give me a fabulous tour of that room and has agreed to assist me in breaking it in after I move in."

I was furious! That son of a bitch was toying with my emotions.

Not catching on, Sandy just laughed, "Paulina is the best."

I walked away, hardly able to keep my composure. It was time to leave. If Blake told Sandy, so be it—I had to get out of there! So I waved goodbye to Sandy and left. On the way out, I noticed Blake staring at me. I gave him a dirty look over my shoulder. At that point, I couldn't stand him or even hide that fact anymore. *He is an arrogant, narcissistic ass!*

When I got home, I poured a glass of wine and started pacing to calm myself down. *If Blake Parker thinks he is going to use this against me, he has another think coming. I will deny it ever happened. If Sandy's cameras were on, she would have already said something, so he has no proof. He has pushed too far and now he has seriously pissed me off. He has no idea how tough I am! I have dealt with the lowest of all humanity, and this arrogant little ass has gone far enough!*

I went to bed angry, and did not sleep well. At 4:30 a.m. I woke and had my coffee on the deck. A few hours later, my phone rang. It was Blake.

"Paulina speaking."

"Good morning, gorgeous."

I quickly cut him off. "What can I do for you?"

"Well, I can think of a few things, but for now I would like to schedule a final walkthrough on the property for tomorrow evening."

I quickly responded in my coldest voice, "Your agent will need to schedule this and will need to accompany you for the walkthrough."

"Chelsea is out of town and won't be back until the morning of the closing."

"Well then, she will need to have one of her associates who is covering her business for her accompany you. I am unavailable, and I represent the seller; this is your agent's responsibility."

Blake paused. "Fine. Thank you for all of your help." I could hear the anger rising in his voice. Apparently he had a temper. He struck me as the type that tried to come off as easy-going when, in reality, there was a rage inside.

I said goodbye and hung up. The closing was in one day, and I was still hoping he would cancel.

I never heard from Chelsea or anyone in her office regarding a final walkthrough.

The morning of the closing, I decided on a black blazer with a white blouse underneath, paired with a black skirt and black heels. I did not wear very much makeup, as I was going for a professional toned-down look. I arrived fifteen minutes early as always and was the first one there, so I introduced myself and was shown into the closing room. Shortly after that, Sandy arrived. Blake and Chelsea were late, but the latter finally showed up looking as striking as she had at the open house. She seemed more like a model than a real estate agent. She greeted us politely.

"Is Mr. Parker is on his way?" I asked.

"Mr. Parker had to leave the country suddenly, so I will be signing for him as power of attorney."

"I see. Does the title company know this?"

"I sent them a copy about an hour ago, and they have their legal team reviewing it. It should not be a problem, as I have signed for him on multiple properties in the past."

Sandy looked concerned. I excused myself and went to talk to the closer, who said briefly, "The POA looks fine and should be approved shortly."

We all waited in awkward silence for another fifteen minutes until the closer came in and told us all was ready to sign.

When all the documents were signed, the closer congratulated Sandy, who looked a little teary. "I did love that house, and there are so many good memories there."

I gave her a hug and said, "You will make new memories in your new home."

The funds were now in Sandy's account. She had been a very wealthy woman beforehand, and now, even more so. I walked her outside and ran to my car. I had a gift basket full of beautiful candle, glasses, and champagne for her. I hugged her again, and we said goodbye.

I was a bit stunned that the closing had just happened. How strange that Blake had not showed up… I didn't believe for one second that he was out of the country.

The check lay on my passenger seat. I settled in behind the wheel, opened the envelope, and stared at the most significant check I had ever seen: $660,000. Enough money for me to finally stop worrying about money. The weird thing was, I didn't feel excited. I felt troubled. It seemed to be both the best and the worst thing that could happen to me.

Money mattered—I knew that firsthand—but, in this case, there was not enough money in the world for me to want to live so near to Blake Parker.

CHAPTER 37
THE BEACH HOUSE

I awoke on Saturday morning and suddenly realized I had $267,000 in the bank. It was almost too much to process. For how rich I felt, it may as well have been a million dollars. I jumped out of bed and ran outside to the patio. I had never felt so happy in my entire life.

The next step was to find a new real estate company. Cody had announced the sale of the business, and the new owners were taking over in one week, so I did not have much time. I hadn't done any research yet, but I knew I wanted to go to one of the best real estate agencies in the city. This sale with Jerry would allow me to get hired wherever I chose. I did a web search and quickly narrowed my options down to two companies. I called them both and set up interviews for Monday. I didn't want to put it off. There would be a lot involved; I would need to notify all of my past clients, print new business cards, update my website, order new signs, and more.

I also wanted to start looking seriously for a home to buy. Now that I had a substantial down payment, I could qualify for something I really wanted. Up until this point, I had not seen anything of interest.

This closing was going to change my life. I felt so grateful towards Jerry; I always knew that he had come into my life for a reason. I didn't believe in accidents, and I knew that God had a plan for me. I also knew in my heart that God was now, finally, answering the prayers that I had prayed almost every day as a child.

I was reflecting on my life and feeling emotional when I heard a text come in. It was from Austin. *Hi darling. I am so excited to see you. I can't stop thinking about you. Would you like to go to my beach house this afternoon, and come back Sunday evening? I think you'll like it there, it's quiet and a great place to relax, and we can celebrate by ourselves and hide away from the world. How does that sound?* I replied, *It sounds perfect. What time should we leave?* Austin replied, *I could pick you up at 1?* I didn't want him to pick me up; I was still embarrassed about my apartment. So I quickly responded, *I could meet you at your house. I'll be in the area.* His answer came in, *Perfect, I can't wait. Kisses!*

Now I'm packing for a stay at a beach house? *Of course he has a beach house... this man has everything.* The thought of spending the whole weekend alone with Austin at a beach house sounded like a fantasy. I felt myself getting more excited by the second as I packed. I shook my head at how seriously I was falling for this man.

I packed two pairs of shorts and two tank tops, my bathing suit, a cute hot pink dress, and my flat sandals. Then I drove to his house, trying not to act too over the moon. When I pulled up, Austin was loading some things into the back of his SUV. He looked up and flashed a big smile. He was wearing off-white shorts and a dark blue shirt with loafers and black sunglasses. I parked and got out of my vehicle, grabbing my suitcase.

Austin reached over and kissed me. "Hi darling, I'm so excited you are here! We are going to have a wonderful weekend!"

I smiled and said, "Yes, we are. Can I help with anything?"

"I got it, honey, I have a few more things inside, and then we can get on the road."

Inside, there was a cooler packed with food, and there was wine and champagne on the counter. Austin had prepared everything. He was always so organized and thoughtful. I loved that about him. I had learned not to count on people, but he seemed like someone who followed through on what he said he would. Everything was packed, and we were ready to go. He turned up the music in the car, and we were on our way. I was happy. Happier than I had been in a long time. Happier then I had ever been in my life.

I was trying my hardest to keep my emotions under control, though. I had never fallen for a man the way I was falling for Austin. He was everything I had ever dreamed of in a man, and the chemistry between us was insane. I was scared. I was certain that relationships never work out, that even the good ones fizzle eventually; and I believed with all of my heart that people always let you down, sooner or later.

Despite these thoughts running through my head, it was a pleasant drive to Austin's beach house, located in a small village tucked away on the water. It was an adorable house with a wrap-around porch where two rocking chairs stood facing the sea. The interior décor was very relaxed with a beachy vibe: whitewashed walls and wood floors with large windows that showcased the view. The furniture was blue and white with comfy pillows. There were three bedrooms and two and a half baths. It was simple but remodeled with quality finishes. The master bedroom was very inviting, with a queen-size bed and a door that led out to the porch and two more chairs on this more private side of the house. I took it all in with delight and said, "This is so cute, I love it! It looks like it straight out of a magazine. Did you decorate it yourself?"

Austin smiled and said, "I did. It was a fixer-upper when I bought it. I worked on it for two years in my spare time, and this is the result. I always wanted a beach house but didn't know where to look for one. So I was hiking one day in this area and spotted this little house. It was vacant and clearly had been neglected for years. I was able to find the owner and made her an offer. It was an elderly woman who had inherited it from her parents. This place is one of my favorite places on earth, you know." He slipped his arms around my waist. "You know where one of my other favorite places on earth is?"

He kissed me on the neck slowly, and I was instantly turned on by his touch. Standing in the master bedroom, he lifted my tank top over my head and slid my shorts to the ground. I slid down to the bed as he stood above me, and we made love. I lost track of time, so lost in the moment with him.

Afterwards, I fell back on the bed and said, "How do you do this to me?"

"Do what?" he said with a little smile.

"I am so attracted to you—all you have to do is kiss me, and I am taking off my clothes!"

"And the problem is?" he laughed and started kissing me again and again.

When we finally managed to leave the bedroom and unpack, we decided to make pasta and a salad for dinner. Afterwards, we shared a bottle of delicious pinot noir on the porch, chatting about work and life. I felt relaxed and was having a great time until he said, "Did you say your family lives in San Francisco?" I froze. It was a lie, the lie I always told, but now it felt strange coming out because I didn't want to lie to Austin. I paused and nodded. I had to stick to the story.

The truth was that my mom, sister, and brother lived in town on the East Side in a low-end subdivision. Patricia had a small apartment of her own and managed to get by but did not have any extra money to really "live." She did not go on vacations, and she didn't drive. In fact she had a phobia of driving, presumably caused by the road rage we all experienced with our dad as children. My mom and brother lived together in a small house. Paul was married for a short time, but he was verbally abusive to his wife, so she left him. All three were barely surviving and deeply affected by the past.

Austin continued, "I travel to San Fran for business regularly. Maybe we can go together sometime. I would love to meet them." My heart sank. The thought of him meeting my family was my worst nightmare. He looked at me and said, "I think you said your father passed away recently?"

I paused again before replying, "Yes."

"That must have been painful for you, I am sorry. How did he die?"

I was starting to get uncomfortable at the questioning. I flashed back to a typical workday a couple of years ago. My phone rang and it was my brother Paul, who rarely called.

"Hi Paul."

"Dad died." He sounded upset. He told me that our father had been in the hospital for the last few weeks and had just died of heart failure. I had not spoken to him in over fifteen years. At this news I felt absolutely nothing at all; it was as if Paul had told me a stranger had died.

So I said, "Okay."

"You need to come down to the funeral home to identify the body. They require all his children to sign a document and they won't cremate him until we do."

"I'm not doing that."

"You have to," Paul demanded in a very aggressive voice.

"I am not doing it, and I don't care what happens to him, I could care less." I meant it. I don't think I ever bonded with my father as a child. Maybe Patricia and Paul did somehow, but I did not. I had no positive feelings towards him nor one good memory of him, not one. Paul hung up, angry.

I was reliving that story, the one I never told anyone, in a silent moment on the porch. Watching me, Austin decided to stop with the questions.

"Well, enough on that depressing subject. Let's talk about my successful girlfriend's latest closing instead."

Girlfriend? So maybe I am his girlfriend?

I smiled. "It was amazing! Jerry and Helena are lovely people and a pleasure to work with. Jerry was one of my very first clients. I helped him with several investment properties and in the process, he taught me a lot about real estate and life. I consider him a friend. The seller was a nice man too... He's going through a divorce. His wife had an affair with a younger man, I guess. Jerry and Helena got a great deal, and the seller even included all the furniture!"

"Wow! I'm glad I have you around to help me with my next real estate deal."

He winked at me and then got up to fetch more wine. We made love again, and I fell asleep in his arms. The next morning, we decided to go for a hike and have a picnic. It was a beautiful day with a slight breeze. We hiked for a couple of hours and then found a lovely spot by a stream.

As we were enjoying our picnic and relaxing, I asked Austin, "So what about your family? Do they live around here?"

Looking down he said, "My parents are both deceased, and I am an only child, so I guess you could say I am alone now."

"I'm so sorry, how did your parents die?"

"My mom died of ovarian cancer, and my dad followed within six months with prostate cancer. I honestly think he died of a broken heart. They were together forty-two years. It was a true love story."

I could see the pain in his eyes. "That is so sad and sweet at the same time. So have you ever been close to finding the kind of love they had?"

Austin paused and said, "I was in a long-term relationship once. She wanted to get married and ultimately gave me an ultimatum to get married, or she was gone. I guess you might say I don't do well with ultimatums. How about you, darling?"

"No, I haven't come close... or had any ultimatums, thank God," I laughed. I added to myself, *I have never even been in love. I've always felt incapable of falling in love until now.*

CHAPTER 38
NEW BEGINNINGS

M y new sole focus was on finding a new real estate office. I was sad; Cody had been not only my mentor, but a friend as well. He'd taught ne everything I knew about the business. But there was no point in putting it off. I had to make this move.

I woke at 5 a.m. on Monday to prepare for my interviews. I picked out a beige skirt that hit just below the knee and paired it a white blouse and low heels. The first person I was scheduled to meet with was a Chloe with Frampton & Associates; they were one of the top real estate companies in the city. I brought my resume. A college degree was glaringly lacking from it, but I did have impressive numbers in sales. The location was downtown in a high-rise. I parked and took the elevator to the top floor, then walked over to the reception desk, where a girl around twenty years old sat. She smiled and said, "May I help you?"

"I'm here to meet Chloe Jacobs. My name is Paulina Paige."

"Yes, please have a seat and she will be with you shortly."

I took a seat and assessed my surroundings. I had always relied on my intuition in high-stakes situations. Immediately I noticed that most of the people working in the office were women and that I liked the décor: the walls were a light gray color, the flooring was a light gray wood. Overall the place had a very contemporary vibe.

Chloe walked around the corner and we made eye contact; she smiled and put out her hand. "Paulina?"

"Yes," I replied. "Nice to meet you."

We walked into her office, and she shut the door. "So, what brings you to Frampton and Associates today?" she asked.

"Well, I am looking for a new office. I have been at Remington Homes for six years, and Better Homes and Gardens recently bought it. I decided this was a good time to make a change."

"Yes, I heard that Cody sold the business. He did a fabulous job of building that business up from the ground. I respect people who work for what they have, and Cody did. Our office is the highest-producing office in the city, and I would like to believe the reason for our success is that we let our agents shine. What I mean by that is, I am not interested in managing anyone. I am here if you have a question, but you are a pro and you can and should run your business as you deem fit. I am not here to motivate you or check on you, I know that you already know how to do that. Otherwise you would not be sitting here today. The bottom line is, I would love to have you join us, and I will offer you the highest commission split we have, which is eighty/twenty. You keep eighty percent. We will provide you with top-of-the-line office support and marketing tools, and you'll have an office on the west side with a view. Does any of that sound of interest to you?"

I was shocked; this was quite an offer! "Yes, it sounds great," I said. "Let me think about it and get back to you."

Chloe smiled and reassured me, "Of course, take as much time as you need. Call me with any questions. I hope to hear from you, Paulina. I think you would fit in excellent with our team and I would be honored to have you here."

"Great, thank you. I will be in touch."

Wow! That went well, I thought as I got in the elevator. *Now on to the next interview.*

The next stop was a company called Schriever and Associates, a well-known company that had a great reputation as a high-end real estate company. The location is in the center of a retail center—the kind of place where customers may walk in off the street. I walked in and looked around. There was no one at the front desk. The office was small but decorated nicely; there was a comfortable, homey vibe to the place. After a minute of waiting, an attractive man noticed me and walked out of his office. "Hi there, can I help you?"

"Yes, I have an appointment with Marsha."

"Okay, she will be right out, please help yourself to a coffee or water."

A few minutes later Marsha walked out. She was around thirty-five and attractive, thin with shoulder-length blonde hair and blue eyes. "Hi Paulina! Come on in."

I followed her to the conference room when we sat down, and she said, "So Paulina, tell me about yourself."

"Well, I have been in the business for about six years and am looking for a new company."

"Do you live in the area?"

"I live about thirty minutes from here."

"Are you married?"

I was starting to dislike the tone of her questioning. "No."

"Do you have any children?"

"No."

"Does your family live close by also?"

I paused and thought, *What does that have to do with job performance?* "My family lives in San Francisco," I stated automatically, and then I decided to take control of the conversation. "Can you tell me a little bit about your company?"

"Um, well, we are the best, and we only hire the best." Then she turned it back around—"Why do you want to work for us?"

I decided right there on the spot that this was not the place for me. I said, "To be honest Marsha, I don't think this is a good fit for me."

"How do you know?" she asked. "You just got here!"

"I just know. Thank you for your time. Have a good day." I got up and walked out.

My decision was made easier than expected: I would join Frampton and Associates.

CHAPTER 39

UNEASY

I was still very uneasy about Blake moving into my neighborhood, but I knew I would have to find a way to let it go and move forward. The money from the closing was a game changer, and I was very grateful. Nevertheless, I didn't see how to shake the dreadful feeling of having to see Blake Parker again in the future.

I had not heard from him, and the closing was now over a month ago. Nor had I not seen him on the beach or in the neighborhood. Curious, I drove by his new house on my way to the office one morning. The house looked abandoned: all the lights were out, and the window coverings remain closed. I wondered why he had not moved in. *What a strange man.*

On a Friday evening, I stopped at the market to pick up a few things for dinner. It was a beautiful evening, and I wanted to eat out on the deck. I was standing in the produce department when I first got a strong feeling that someone was looking at me. I turned but didn't see anyone. The creepy feeling lingered, though. I quickly grabbed a few items and went to the check-out stand, looking over my shoulder for anyone I might recognize. I didn't notice anything or anyone suspicious. I quickly went to my car, checking the backseat first, and drove straight home. I'd been planning to drive to the liquor store as well, but I didn't want to stop anywhere now. I just wanted to get back home.

When I pulled in to the garage, I looked around before getting out and then quickly ran into the house and locked the door behind me. I was freaked out. I had lived in this home for a couple of years now and never felt scared. It was a very safe neighborhood, the kind of community where people looked out for each other. I told myself I was just being paranoid and poured a glass of wine which I took out to the deck. The sun was setting over the ocean, and it was a picture-perfect evening. I reminded myself of how lucky I was to live here and started to relax.

I opened up the grill to barbeque the salmon I'd picked up. The salmon was cooking, and I was enjoying the view when I noticed someone walking on the beach alone. They were strolling with their head hanging down. It seemed odd. It was the kind of walk that made you wonder if something was wrong with them—slow, with a depressed vibe. I decided to get my binoculars and take a closer look. I went inside to get them, and when I came back the person was gone. I looked and looked, and there was no sight of them. This was even more strange, because there was nowhere they could've gone but into someone's backyard. The houses that backed to the beach were typically gated and always fenced, so how this person simply vanished from the middle of the beach made no sense.

It had been a bizarre evening, and my unease was at a high again. I quickly finished cooking the salmon and went in, locking the deck's sliding doors as I passed through. I usually kept them open; no one could get in by this door, as the deck was hundreds of feet from the ground. But that night, I just felt safer with them secured. That may have been the first time I ever locked them since I'd moved into the house. I went into the bedroom and decided to read for a while. I was tired but unable to sleep. I finally fell into a troubled, restless doze.

CHAPTER 40

DREAMS

I was excited but also a little nervous to start working at Frampton and Associates. I knew it was the right time to make the change but was still sad to part from Cody. On my last day at Remington Homes, I asked him to meet for lunch. We reminisced about the past and got teary when we hugged and said goodbye. We agreed to keep in touch, though I wondered if it would actually happen.

Then it was my first day at Frampton and Associates. Chloe was in the reception area when I came in with my laptop and a few files, and she came over and gave me a hug. "Welcome! Let me show you your office." We walked down the hall and turned left. I was speechless—it was a large office with amazing views. The windows overlooked the entire city and the water. Chloe continued, "I brought in an extra filing cabinet. If you need anything at all, let me know. I would love to go for a drink sometime when you get settled." She smiled and was gone.

I sat down at the desk and faced my spectacular view, took a deep breath, and said a prayer. *Thank you, God. You have blessed me in so many ways.* I sat there for a few minutes more, and then thought, *I need to get to work and make some money! After all, I do work on straight commission.*

After lunch, I decided to call my former clients to let them know I had relocated. I decided to start with Jerry. He answered on the second ring.

"Hi Paulina."

"Hello Jerry, how are you?"

"Good, thank you."

"How is everything going with the new house?" It had been over a month since we closed on the house on Village Road.

"It is going well, we have moved in and are getting settled. Riley and Samantha are moved into our house and the baby is due in a few months."

"Wow that is exciting! How do you like your neighborhood?"

"It seems great. The neighbors are nice but not too nosy."

"Wonderful," I laughed.

"Thank you for the beautiful piece of art," Jerry said, "Helena and I enjoy it very much."

"You're very welcome!... I called to let you know I have switched real estate companies. I'm with Frampton and Associates now."

"Congratulations! That is a smart move. You have outgrown Remington Homes."

"Thank you, Jerry. Tell Helena I said hi and let's keep in touch!"

I hung up the phone. *I am going to miss him... he probably won't be needing my services now for a long time.* For once, I was actually going to try and keep in touch. Jerry had been such an influence in my life, and I would always be grateful that I met him. I believed that people come into our lives to teach us lessons and guide us, and I had no doubt that Jerry and I met to help each other. I wasn't sure how much I taught him, but he certainly changed my entire life.

As I adjusted to my new company, I was actively looking for a house to purchase. Soon a new listing hit the market that caught my eye—a townhome in a neighborhood called Prado Terrace. It was smaller than I was hoping for, but the owner had completely remodeled the home, and the finishes were beautiful. There were two bedrooms and three bathrooms, a two-car attached garage, and a large deck. The price was $599,000. If I were to put down $200,000 from my closing with Jerry, I could afford the payment. I set a showing and went to see it immediately. The moment I walked in, I knew this was where I was supposed to be. I went back to the office and prepared an offer for $575,000 and a quick closing of three weeks. The seller accepted my offer, and I was under contract in no time. I was nearly bouncing in excitement, so I called Austin on my way home to share my win.

"Hi darling."

"Hello, I have great news!"

"Oh, tell me."

"I am under contract on a townhome!"

"Wow, that's exciting, when can I see it?"

"How about tomorrow?"

"That is perfect, and then we can go out and celebrate! Kisses."

I went home and looked around my apartment; it was a small one-bedroom with old furniture. I had outgrown this place on so many levels. It was high time for a change. I poured myself a glass of wine and put on some music, and soon found myself dancing and singing to the Rolling Stones, my favorite band. Life was good.

The next day Austin met me at the property. He grabbed me and held me close with a, "Hi gorgeous!" As we approached the building, he paused and looked around, carefully observing the exterior and grounds. After we got buzzed in the door, we took the elevator to the seventh floor, which was third from the top. From the windows overlooking the deck we could see a peek of the water in the distance. Austin quietly looked at each room and then stood out on the deck silently for a minute. Then he looked over and said, "I like it. I think it will be a good investment for you. I am happy for you, honey."

I could tell that he meant it. I beamed and said, "Thank you! Let's go celebrate."

We went to a restaurant on the water and sat outside. Austin ordered a bottle of champagne and made a toast. "To your beautiful new home. May it bring you happiness, peace, and love."

This man always makes the best toasts and has a way with words. Is it possible for him to actually be this wonderful? I was waiting for the other shoe to drop. It seemed too good to be true; once he found out about my past and family, I was sure, he would look down on me and we would be over. He came from a healthy family with parents who stayed married for forty-plus years—he would be horrified when he found out my truth. I had better not get too close and just enjoy it while it lasted.

We went back to his house and sat outside soaking in the beautiful evening. From our chairs side by side, he reached over and held my hand. He didn't say anything, just held my hand. No one had ever done that before. I got up and stood in front of him and he slowly undressed me, and we made love on the grass. I have never had sex like that; it was so sensual and erotic. I loved the feeling of the green grass and the fresh air blowing softly on my skin as we touched. *I am in over my head with this one,* I reminded myself again. *I have to keep my distance no matter what, because sooner or later it will end!*

CHAPTER 41
UNANSWERED QUESTIONS

I lay in bed as dawn broke, listening to the sound of the ocean and thinking about the feeling I'd gotten at the market and the person I'd seen walking on the beach. The oddness of it all was more than just creepy, it was almost scary. Speaking of creepy and scary, Blake crossed my mind again. Still no sign of him since before closing. Strange indeed.

I decided to go for a run. I had been avoiding the beach in case Blake was in the area, but I knew I couldn't live in this weird limbo forever and had to get back to my routine. It seemed so odd that he hadn't moved in... *Who buys a $20-million home and lets it sit empty? Everything about him is strange.* I grabbed my headphones and headed out to the beach, where I sped up into a run. I was about a mile in when I noticed someone sitting on the deck of one of the oceanside houses whose owner I didn't know. It was a man, and he was staring at me. I could not make out his features; he was too far away. But I could tell he never took his eyes off of me. I kept running and then slowed to a walk, then decided to turn around and head back home. I looked over my shoulder, and the man was gone. It was a little eerie. *What is going on? I must be paranoid... maybe I am reading into meaningless details?!*

At home I turned on some music and started cleaning. I was just starting to feel better when my phone rang. I did not recognize the number, but I answered anyway. "Paulina speaking." The other end was quiet, and then the line went dead. I dialed the number back, and it just rang—there was no voicemail. *Must've been a wrong number,* I thought. I continued cleaning and felt tense.

I was having a busy week at work. I started working with a new client who was relocating from New Jersey. He was looking for a home for himself and his family, and his wife was planning to come out the following week to help him view properties.

Also, I received an invitation from one of my neighbors to a party at their house Friday night. I decided to go. I knew that Blake might be present, but he had not even moved in, so I thought it unlikely. If he was there, I would leave and make up some excuse about an emergency I needed to attend to. I needed to get out, and networking with the neighbors was how I got my business.

On Friday afternoon, I put on my white dress with black heels. I was fairly confident that Blake wouldn't be there; I had assured myself by driving past his new house several times and observing that he hadn't moved in.

I arrived at the party and brought a bottle of wine as a gift for the hosts. Their names were Pat and Patty, and they were a sweet couple in their sixties. Pat used to work in the stock market on Wall Street and made millions, and Patty was a stay-at-home mom. They were friendly and liked to party, so they hosted several get-togethers each year. When I walked in, the very first thing I noticed was Chelsea. My heart dropped. If she was here, then *he* probably was too. I glanced around but did not see him. When Chelsea spotted me the next instant, I turned away quickly. I went to the bar and ordered a martini. I chatted with a couple of neighbors, and when I turned around, she was standing there, looking stunning. She was skinny with long dark hair with beautiful brown eyes and olive skin. She was wearing a tight black dress that showed off her perfect body and very high black heels.

"Paulina, how are you?" she said warmly, like we were best friends.

I stuttered slightly and said, "H—hi, how are you?"

Chelsea chatted a bit about traveling and how busy life had been, and I waited for a chance to ask her the question on my mind.

"So, is Blake going to move into his new house?"

She laughed, "I'm sure he will eventually. He has been traveling in Europe."

"I see."

"It was nice to see you, Paulina, take care." Then she turned and left.

It seemed strange to see her there; I assumed she must have known Pat and Patty. I stayed for about an hour longer and then left.

As I got in my car, I noticed a car tucked away behind some bushes. It looked rather out of place, but I could not see the full thing, so I couldn't tell what make or model it was. I drove off with an unsettled feeling and was happy to get home.

CHAPTER 42
THE BEGINNING OF THE END

I was falling hard for Austin. Keeping my emotions in check was becoming more and more difficult; I loved sleeping with him, both figuratively and literally. We got along great and never argued, though we were spending more and more time together.

I was doing well at Frampton and Associates. I was not the top agent—there were some really heavy hitters in the office—but I did well and was paying extra towards the principal on my townhome loan every month. I liked Chloe, and we were starting to become friends. We would go to happy hour together and out to lunch regularly. She never acted like my boss, nor did she push me to produce more sales. She liked me, and we clicked.

Austin was traveling more than usual. He had clients in Portland and L.A. whom he had to visit once a week. On a Friday evening he and I were having dinner at one of our favorite restaurants in La Jolla. Seated upstairs on the deck overlooking the water, we were basking in the warmth of the fire pit near our table. Austin commented, "I hired a new employee today to help me with all the traveling. Her name is Elizabeth."

Something about the way he said her name made my heart sink. I sensed something right away. "Oh, tell me about her," I said, trying to ignore the alarm ringing in my brain.

"She has tons of experience. She used to work for Merrill Lynch and was the VP in Europe. She has a master's degree in finance and has traded millions of dollars on Wall Street. She has a great personality that I think will work well with our clients. She's willing to travel with me, and eventually will travel solo, freeing up my time."

I felt ill. I knew this was the turning point in our relationship; in fact, this was the other shoe dropping, so to speak. I had been waiting for it, and here it was. This woman was smart—not just a little smart, but really smart and highly educated—and everything else I was not. Austin would fall for her. This was the kind of woman he wanted to be with and deserved. She was the type everyone was expecting him to date. I was devastated, like it had already happened and we were over. As soon as I could find my voice, I said, "What's her last name?" I thought to myself, *I need to Google her and see just how attractive she is.*

Austin looked at me kind of strangely and said, "Franklin, why? Do you think you might know her?"

I tried to smile but couldn't. "No, I am just curious. When does she start?"

"She's going with me to L.A. on Monday."

Wow, just like that. In my mind and heart, I could feel it. I quickly responded, "Well, we should go. We both have a busy week next week."

Austin took my hand. "Next week? What about now and this weekend? Let's enjoy it."

But I couldn't stand being with him one more second. "I really should go, I have some things to do for work. I am going to go."

Austin looked surprised. "Okay, let me get the check."

"I'll grab an Uber. Bye."

I ran outside, fighting back the tears, grabbed a ride, and went straight home. I could barely make it in the apartment before I broke down sobbing. My heart was breaking. I tried to tell myself that nothing has happened yet, that he had only just hired her. Maybe she was married, for all I knew. It didn't matter, though. I knew where it would go. I scolded myself for becoming so invested in the relationship; I'd always known I could not trust anyone, especially with my heart. It hit me right then like a slap: *I am in love with Austin.* I cried harder than I had in years.

I finally calmed down enough to Google the name Elizabeth Franklin. *Such an intelligent name.* Immediately several pictures and profiles popped up, all work-related, and one article about her from the Wall Street Journal. She was a brunette, tall, and thin, and seemed to wear very little makeup. She was attractive, not gorgeous or flashy, but charming and very smart looking. I read some more; it looked like she was not married. I decided this was the one that would tear us apart. I was an emotional mess. My phone rang. It was from Austin. I let it go to voicemail.

"Hi, darling. Are you okay? I'm worried and I don't know what happened at dinner... Call me. Miss you. Kisses."

More tears flowed. I was a wreck. I kept trying to tell myself I was overreacting. Austin hadn't done anything wrong yet. But I just knew they would click and he would fall for her. How could he not? She was so smart, and they would be traveling together and going out to dinner in close company; it was just a matter of time before it happened. I should have known better to fall for him. I'd been expecting it would end once he found out about my childhood and family, all the secrets I'd been keeping since we met. Once that happened, he would never forgive me. So it would be better to end it like this, before the lying became evident. My heart felt like it was breaking into a thousand pieces.

A text came in from Austin—*Hi darling, I am concerned, would you like me to come over?* The thought of him coming over was my worst nightmare. I responded, *No, I'm not feeling well, but I will be fine. I need some rest.* A minute later—*Okay, let me know if you need anything. I miss you. Kisses.*

I had to figure out the best way to get out of this relationship. I went into my bedroom and lay on my bed to cry myself to sleep.

When I woke up in the morning, it was eight. I never slept so late. I still had my clothes on from the day before, and I hadn't washed my makeup off, so I had black rings of mascara under my eyes. I looked at myself in the mirror and thought, *You have to pull yourself together, girl!*

I made some coffee and looked around the apartment. I had started packing, and there were boxes everywhere. The closing was next week. So I decided I wasn't leaving the house until I had finished packing. I would avoid Austin and focus on the move.

He called at nine. "Good morning, beautiful. How are you?"

I tried to sound reasonable. "Good morning, I am fine, how are you?"

"I'm good. You're feeling better, darling?"

"Yes, I am."

"I'm glad to hear that, I thought we could go out on the water today, and then you can come over, and I will make you a delicious dinner. Yes?"

It sounded amazing, but I knew I had to start pulling away slowly so as not to be too obvious. "It sounds great, but I need to finish packing this weekend so I can be ready for the move next week."

"I can help you," Austin offered.

"No thank you, I have it under control."

"Okay, well… let me know if there is anything I can do or if you need anything. I guess I'll see you next weekend because I'm out of town the whole week. If you have any problems with the movers, let me know, and I'll get someone to help you right away."

"Thank you. Talk to you later."

He paused. "Okay. Kisses."

I hung up feeling sad and empty, but I knew I had to do this. It would be even worse if I waited. At least this way, I would be in control of how it ended. I wiped away a few tears and started packing.

Chapter 43

More Clues

I had always loved living in Bel Air Estates; it still felt like a dream. It had always felt so safe and welcoming that I had never worried about living alone. Up until recently, that is.

On a peaceful Sunday morning I was driving past Blake's house. It appeared he had still not moved in. There were no cars parked outside, and all the blinds were securely closed just as they had been every time I'd made a drive by. It had been six months since the closing, and I still hadn't sighted him once. How long would he let this house sit empty? I slowly drove off and was halfway down the street when, in my rear view mirror, I spotted a car pulling into the driveway of Blake's house. My heart started to race. I didn't want to be too obvious, so I kept going and parked at the end of the road, then turned in my seat to peer at the car. It was a new Mercedes, a dark gray sport model sedan. It parked in the driveway and a woman stepped out. It was Chelsea! She walked to the front door and opened the door with a key. I was so confused; what could she be doing there? I waited for a few minutes and then left. *Maybe she is just checking on things?* I went back home and decided to keep an eye out. I was curious as to exactly what was going on.

While working in my office, I decided to Google Blake again. Perhaps I'd missed something the first time I looked him up. I scrolled through multiple results, and then I saw something that made me stop—a photo of him. He looked younger, so it must have been at least a few years old. He was very good looking, even better than he was now. The woman he was standing next to was attractive but older; she seemed to be about fifty. They were at a party or event. As I examined the picture, I found that the background looked familiar... *It looks like my deck! The hot tub and the deck railing, exactly like mine... This photo was definitely taken at my house!* Then I remembered what Sandy told me about Blake: he lived in my house years ago with the original owners. I continued to search for information, and I found another picture of the woman he was with. Tanya Weaver. At the time of the photograph, she was married to Thomas Weaver. I knew who Thomas Weaver was, of course, but had never seen his wife. Blake and Tanya looked very cozy together, and I had a feeling they were more than just friends. After much more Googling, I confirmed that Tanya and Thomas divorced. *This Blake character gets around!*

I found Tanya's Facebook profile. She had never remarried. There were photos of her and Blake on her page, but they were not recent; her newest ones revealed a much different person. She was looking older and a little heavier and not very happy. Most were with her dog. Compared to the first picture of her and Blake, she looked like a completely different person.

I was more curious than ever now about Blake. *What is his story, and where is he?... I suppose I should just be thankful that I haven't had to see him.*

I spent the rest of the day around the house and then decided to go shopping. I needed to pick up some makeup, so I drove up to Macy's. It was crowded, which was why I usually avoided it on the weekends. I was browsing around when I noticed a woman looking at me from across several aisles. She was wearing a large-brimmed hat and a tan dress. I didn't recognize her. I continued to shop but could feel her staring at me. Soon she walked over to me, and I said hello.

She stared at me as though studying every feature. "Are you Paulina Page?"

"Yes, I am. Who are you?"

"My name is Virginia, and I live in Bel Air Estates. Do you know Blake Parker?"

"We're acquainted, why?"

"He has approached me about purchasing my house. One of my friends said that he just bought another home in the area and I think you may have been the realtor."

"Yes, that is correct. Which house is yours, if you don't mind me asking?"

"It is on Village Road, overlooking the ocean."

"Oh yes, we are neighbors. I live on Village Road as well." I wanted to find out more. "So, does Blake want to buy your home to live in?"

"Yes, he said he likes the area. My friend said I should ask you if he is legit or just wasting time. I don't think I want to sell, but I was curious about what you could tell me about him."

"I don't know him well. I was representing the seller on the home that he purchased. I'm sorry I can't be of more help. Good day." I turned and left. My mind was racing. *So Blake is still around! In fact, he is nearby. Why would he buy another house when he has not moved into the first one?*

I was fairly certain of which house was Virginia's; it was just down the beach from mine. I had not been there, but I passed by when I ran on the beach. If Blake did buy this house, he would be almost next door. The thought made me feel ill. Virginia said she didn't think she wanted to sell; I hoped this was true.

CHAPTER 44

CELEBRATING

A s I prepared for the move, I found it impossible to keep my mind off Austin. My imagination was running wild with thoughts of him in L.A. with Elizabeth. I couldn't shake the image of them having dinner together and then sex. I was an emotional wreck.

I continued to pack for the closing tomorrow at 9 a.m. I would move right away. I worked the rest of the day and got close to finishing; it would be mostly the big things left to move after all the boxes were out. The apartment looked old and run-down to me, and I was ready to be out of there. It had served its purpose, but I had outgrown it on many levels. I went to bed early feeling uptight—I hadn't heard anything from Austin all day, which confirmed that he and Elizabeth were hitting it off. I finally fell into a restless sleep.

I awoke at 6 a.m. *My big day is here! Closing and moving day!* I tried to push Austin out of my mind with my excitement. Dressed in a red dress and black heels—red is a power color, so I thought that was appropriate—I arrived early. I was the first one there and went into the closing room to wait. The closer came in shortly, and then the seller and the listing broker. The seller was a young man, around twenty. Very young to own this property. He smiled at me and said, "Hey." The listing broker was around thirty and had a pleasant look about her, straight blonde hair and no makeup. She smiled and greeted me as well. I asked the young man if he enjoyed living there.

"Yeah, it was cool. I'm moving to a house on the beach so I can surf more."

Ah, a trust fund baby. Must be nice, I thought to myself.

Everything went well; all the paperwork was signed, and the seller handed me the keys. "Enjoy. Have a good one." He got up and left.

Then they were all gone, and I was standing there holding the keys to the first home I had ever purchased. It was a very surreal feeling. I wanted so much to share it with Austin—then I remembered that it was over. I felt the tears rise to my eyes. It took everything I had to hold them back as I walked out, choked out a "thank you" to the receptionist, and got in the car; and then the tears flowed. I felt such a loss thinking about not being able to share this moment with Austin.

To cheer myself up, I drove to my new place. I didn't have any of my things, and I had to meet the movers in a couple of hours, but I just wanted to see it again. I parked in the front and walked right in using the security sensor on the key ring. I went to the seventh floor, opened my front door, and gazed around. *I can't believe this is my house. I am so happy and so proud!* I explored every room again. My joy was so overwhelming that the thoughts of Austin faded a bit. Then I heard a knock—it was a delivery man standing there with a beautiful bouquet of flowers.

"These are for Paulina."

"Yes, that's me." I took the flowers and closed the door. The card read: *Paulina, Congratulations on your new home! I am so proud of you and your success. I hope it brings you everything your heart desires. I can't wait to celebrate. Love Austin. Kisses.*

"Love"? That was the first time he has ever used that word, and it freaked me out. Why was he making this so hard for me?

I wanted to see him. I missed him. *Maybe I could be with him one more time?* Quickly, I called him before I changed my mind. But the call went to voicemail. Just hearing his recorded voice made me nervous, so I left a terse message—terser than I meant to. "Hi, thank you for the flowers. Bye." I hung up and felt strange. *What an immature message. Calm down, Paulina.*

I drove back home and arrived just as the movers were pulling in. They came in and started loading up. I was filling my car with things as well and would follow them over. All full up, we headed to my new home. After two more trips, we were done. The movers, whom Austin had recommended to me, did an excellent job. I paid them and went inside to face my things, which were scattered about everywhere. I had to organize and clean up, but it felt perfect. I had an excellent feeling about this place. As I unpacked, I popped open some champagne. Just because I was alone didn't mean I couldn't celebrate. I started with some boxes and made the bed, then sat down on the deck. My mind went straight to Austin. It was 7 p.m., so he was probably out to dinner with Elizabeth. I was picturing the scene with a darkened mood when my phone rang. It was him.

"Hi, darling! Congratulations! How's everything going?"

"Hi, it's going well. Everything is moved in, but it's a mess. I have a lot of work to do. How are you?"

"All is good, we are keeping busy. I can't wait to see you. I will call you tomorrow. Goodnight, kisses."

I hung up, allowing myself to see him one more time once he got back. I missed him so much. But after that, I would have to cut it off. I drank the rest of the champagne and danced and sang in my new living room. *I can't believe this is* my *living room!*

CHAPTER 45
NO MEANS NO

I passed by Blake's house again on the way home from the mall. As usual, all the blinds were closed and the lights were off. I'd never seen the lights on since he purchased the house. The yard was starting to look neglected; the grass and flowers were dying. When I got home, I turned on some music and was considering what to cook for dinner when the phone rang. It was Sandy.

"Hi Sandy! How are you?"

"I am well, thank you, Paulina. I wanted to ask you if you know anything about that Blake character who bought my house?"

"Not really, why?"

"Well, it appears that he has never moved in and the house is deteriorating, just sitting empty."

"I noticed that too, I have driven by a few times. I have no idea why he hasn't moved in. I haven't seen or heard from him since before the closing."

"Very strange… Well, if you hear anything let me know. I hate to see that house get neglected. Charles and I loved it with all our hearts."

"I understand. Have a good night."

"Goodbye."

So word was out, and people were starting to wonder. I started dinner and decided to watch a movie, something light—maybe a chick flick. Once I finished my delicious mahi-mahi, I settled in on the couch. I was relaxed and almost asleep when the phone rang. My heart skipped a beat when I saw it was Blake.

"Hello?"

"Hi beautiful. It has been too long. I would love to see you."

I was shocked. *After all this time, he called to hit on me?!* I responded, "Blake, I thought I made myself clear months ago that what happened between us was a mistake. I am not interested in dating you."

"'Dating'? Who said we have to date? I want to have sex with you, I want to have my way with you, I want a repeat of the recreation room tour. And I want it soon."

I was temporarily speechless, taken aback by his bold, arrogant attitude. Finally I said, "That is not going to happen. I do have a question for you, though—are you planning to move into your new house?"

Blake laughed and said, "Only if you will meet me in the rec room. Do we have a deal?"

"No, we do not."

"I see. Well then, I better let you go. Take care of your beautiful self, Paulina." He hung up.

I felt sick to my stomach. If I ever heard from him again, I might get a restraining order. *He creeps me out and I wish had never met him; I would give up my commission in a heartbeat if I could take all of it back. I regret that disgusting mistake and every word spoken between me and Blake Parker.*

CHAPTER 46
CAN'T LET GO

I had made significant progress in unpacking and adjusting into my new townhome by that Friday. Austin was back in town that day, but I hadn't made any definite plans with him yet. I still wanted to see him one last time before I ended it.

I was hanging a few pictures when I heard a knock on the door. It took me by surprise; I was not expecting anyone. I looked out the peephole and saw Austin. Caught off guard, I glanced in the mirror I had hung up by the front door. I looked rough—very little makeup and my hair pulled back in a ponytail, and I was wearing my workout clothes. I thought about not answering, but he knew I was home. My car was parked outside. I opened the door.

"Hi darling!" He grabbed me and kissed me. His touch felt so good. I hugged him and held on for a second. Then he walked in and looked around. "Wow, you have been busy! The place is looking great. I can help you, but we have to celebrate first!"

He reached for me and laid his lips on mine again. His hands were moving all over my body, and in a moment he had slipped off my workout shorts. He slid his hand up my thigh and started touching me soft and slow, as he kept kissing me. I was unbearably turned on. I took off my top and unbuttoned his shirt and unzip his pants, and then we made love on the living room floor.

I am crazy about this man. How am I ever going to break it off? I'm addicted to his touch and can't imagine not seeing or feeling him. I decided to not think about it; for now, I would focus on getting settled into my place.

We both got dressed and went out to the deck. Austin looked at me and said, "I missed you."

That made me squirm uncomfortably. An hour ago I was ready to break it off, and now I just had sex with him and we were cuddling on the deck. "How did it go with Elizabeth?" I asked.

"It went well. I think she will work out great, and then I can travel less. I would rather be here with you."

This made me feel better, and I decided to let it go for now. He stayed with me at my new place that night and helped me move some of the heavy furniture items and hang some wall art. After working for several hours we ordered Chinese takeout and ate it out on the deck with a bottle of Chardonnay. Then we made love again, and I fell asleep in his arms.

CHAPTER 47

LOSS

Time passed, and Austin and I were still spending every weekend together; we took turns staying at my house, his house, and his beach house. I tried not to think about Elizabeth, but I knew that eventually, Austin would fall for her. My belief that people could not be trusted was unshaken.

It was a hazy, dark Monday with a chilly breeze in the air. The forecast called for rain. It was one of those mornings when you don't want to get out of bed. I woke up at 7 a.m., made a cup of coffee, and went into my office to plan my day. I had a busy afternoon and would need to drive into the city to meet a client first. After a quick spin class, I jumped in the shower. I decided on a pair of black slacks and a white blouse. I didn't wear pants very often—I was a skirt and dress girl all the way—but with the dreary weather, it felt right. I was on the highway by 10 a.m., headed to my 11:30 appointment. A call came in from an unknown number.

"Paulina speaking."

There was a pause. "Hi, this is Riley Newman."

The name sounded familiar. Within a couple of seconds I knew who it was—Jerry's son. I had never met him, but Jerry had spoken of him often.

Riley's voice was low as he continued. "My parents Jerry and Helena Newman were killed in a car accident. My father spoke of you often, so I thought you would like to know."

I felt like someone kicked me in the stomach. I veered, almost losing control of the wheel. I couldn't speak. We held a silence. Finally, I choked, "Oh my god, I am so sorry. I'm so sorry. When?" I could barely get the words out.

"Two days ago. The service will be this week. I can let you know when and where."

"Yes, please." That is all I could say before the tears started flowing.

Riley said, "Okay," and hung up.

Shaking, I got off at the next exit. I pulled into a gas station and sobbed hysterically. I had never lost anyone before, and Jerry wasn't just my friend, he was also a father figure to me. He was the father that I never had. I thought about the last time that I talked to him and the last thing I said. "Let's keep in touch." I hadn't kept in touch.

I am an idiot! The closest person I had to a real father. A real friend. The person who influenced and changed my life more than any other... and I didn't keep in touch.

Trembling uncontrollably and hiding my face in my minds, I sat at the gas station for at least thirty minutes before trying to pull myself together. I realized I was late for my appointment and managed to dial Chloe. As soon as she picked up I said, "Chloe, there has been an emergency, please cancel my appointment."

"Are you okay?"

"There has been a death in my family." The words came out of my mouth automatically. To me, Jerry was family. The kind of family I had always wanted but never had for real.

Shocked, Chloe exclaimed, "I am so sorry! Of course, I'll take care of the appointment. Please let me know how I can help."

I drove home in silence, trying to hold myself together. The weather was tempestuous—pouring rain and windy. It was the worst day of my life. I went inside, changed into my pajamas, and crumpled onto the couch. *How did this happen?* I thought about Helena, so beautiful and full of life. It was impossible to believe they were both gone, just like that.

I turned on my laptop and Googled traffic accidents in the last few days. I didn't watch television or listen to the local news, so it was not surprising that I hadn't heard anything. I found the news story almost instantly. Apparently Jerry and Helena were traveling on Highway 101 on Saturday afternoon, Jerry in the driver's seat. There was construction on the road that had been going on for a while, and it was raining. The car hydroplaned into the next lane, directly into a semi. The report said Jerry died on contact, while Helena was airlifted to Scripps Memorial Hospital and died within an hour of arrival, having lost too much blood. Horrified, I pictured the scene in my mind. *How could this happen so fast? One second they are here, and then they're gone forever.*

I thought about Riley and his wife and baby. Jerry was always concerned that Samantha didn't really love his son and only wanted his money; now neither parent was here to look after Riley. I felt a need to do something, to help somehow, but I didn't know how.

My mind was racing, and I was crying and shaking once more. I retreated to bed with swollen eyes, just replaying the scene in my head over and over again. I could see Jerry and Helena's faces and the terrible moment of the crash. I couldn't shake the image of their crushed car. I cried myself to sleep.

I woke up at 5:30 a.m. and lay in bed thinking about the call from Riley. His voice had sounded so weak and faint. Jerry had shown me a picture of Riley years ago from when he was a child before the accident, and another picture of him after the accident. He was a cute kid with dark brown hair and brown eyes. After the accident, his personality had changed; he became more introverted and barely spoke. He was now twenty-five and his baby was ten months. The last time I talked to Jerry, the baby was not born yet and the future was bright; Riley and Samantha had moved into Jerry and Helena's old house, and they were preparing for the birth. Now life had taken a tragic turn, and everything was changed forever. I would never forgive myself for not keeping in touch with Jerry. I guess I foolishly thought he would always be there.

I canceled all my appointments for the rest of the week, as I was in no condition to work. Soon Austin texted me, *Good morning, darling. Would you like to go for a sunset cruise tonight? I miss you.* I replied, *My friend Jerry and his wife Helena died in a car accident. I am not okay.*

He called immediately. "Honey, what can I do for you?"

"I don't know," I replied. "I need some time. I will call you later."

"Can I come over and be with you? I will cancel my appointments."

"No, I need to be alone."

"Okay, please let me know if I can do anything. I am so sorry. I love you."

Oh my god! Did he just say the L-word? I froze and couldn't say anything. I finally said, "Okay. Goodbye."

Why would he say this to me, and especially now? I'm a wreck! Lord knows I don't need him to start throwing around the "L" word!

I had never told anyone that I love them. No one, not one person in my whole life. I was not about to start now. And no one had told me they loved me before either. "Love" was not a word used in my family. Ever.

I tried to get some work done but couldn't see through my tears. I went for a walk outside but broke down and had to return. So I went to bed in early evening, exhausted and unable to function.

The next morning Chloe texted me. *Paulina are you ok? Thinking about you, so sorry for your loss. If I can do anything, please let me know.* I sent a brief text to thank her.

On Wednesday I called Riley. I had saved his number on my phone. He answered in a low voice.

"Hello."

"Hi Riley, this is Paulina Paige. I wanted to check in and see if there is anything I can do to help. I know you don't know me, but I want to help. I know you and Samantha have a baby and I can only imagine how difficult this time is, so please let me help. I can babysit, I can cook, clean, shop, anything you need."

Riley hesitated and then said quietly, "No thanks. The service is on Friday at 2 p.m. at Saint Petersburg Church, if you would like to come."

"Yes, I will be there. Please let me know if I can help in any way."

Riley hung up.

I felt empty and so alone. I could tell he was not going to let me in. At least, not yet. I stayed at home, barely eating or sleeping. Austin called several times offering to help, but I told him I needed some time. Thank God he didn't push it and show up at my door. I wouldn't have been able to handle that.

Friday morning, I knew I had to prepare for the hardest day of my life. I felt like I needed to speak at the service. I had no idea what exactly to say, but it was my last chance to tell Jerry how I felt. But was I even allowed to speak? I called Riley again.

He answered in the same monotone voice. "Hello."

"Riley, this is Paulina. I would like to know if I may speak at the service?"

Riley paused and said, "Okay."

I replied, "Thank you. I look forward to meeting you. I have heard so much about you over the years."

Riley paused and said, "Okay, goodbye." He sounded like a zombie. He was probably in shock and might need medication.

As I got ready to leave, I prayed, *Dear God, please give me strength, I cannot do this without you. Please help me to find the words to say and show me how to help Riley and his wife and baby. I know Jerry and Helena are with you. Please tell them I miss them, and I am sorry I did not keep in touch. I will never forgive myself for that. Amen.*

I wore a long black skirt and black blouse. I had never been to a funeral in my life, but I knew you're supposed to wear black. I put on very little makeup and no jewelry. My hair I left straight; I couldn't bring myself to curl it. My eyes were bloodshot and baggy. I had never looked worse in my life. In fact, I looked like a different person than I had just five days ago, and the truth was, I *was* different.

I walked into a very crowded church and faced the daunting task of finding a seat. I was standing in the back looking around and starting to panic—*I should have gotten here earlier*—when I spotted Riley the front row. I recognized him from the photos. From his seat in the pew, he seemed to know it was me and waved at me to come up front. He had saved me a seat. I almost burst into tears but managed to keep my composure as I walked to the front. Samantha was sitting next to Riley, holding their infant son. I stood there with my arms out to hug Riley, but he just looked down. So I awkwardly bent over and hugged him lightly, and Samantha as well, and sat down. Up on the stage, there were several pictures; one of Jerry, one of Helena, and one of them together with Riley when he was younger, before the accident. That was it. The second I saw Jerry's face, I lost it. I was crying and shaking. The service had not even started yet, and I couldn't keep it together.

The minister soon came out and started the service, first by reading a poem and following it with a Bible Scripture. When he stopped talking, Riley stood up to walk to the stage. Hunched over, he stepped hard on his prosthetic leg, which was covered by tan slacks, while sliding the other leg along behind him. He slowly adjusted the microphone to his height, cleared his voice, and in a very meek, low voice, said, "Mom and Dad, I'm sorry for the things I did to make your lives harder. The accident I had was my own fault, I was driving too fast and acting as a show-off. Thank you for everything. I will try to do better in life. I love you." With cracking voice and fighting back the tears, he slowly shuffled off the stage.

Then the minister walked up again and asked, "Is there anyone else who would like to speak?" There was silence. I knew this was it— I had to do it now. I slowly stood and went to the stage, praying, *Please God help me.* I approached the microphone and closed my eyes, gathering my thoughts. After a few seconds that felt like an eternity, I spoke.

"Many years ago, I met Jerry Newman. He was the kindest, most intelligent man I have ever met. He taught me so much about life, and he taught me in a gentle, reassuring way. I always felt like he was a father to me, the father I never had. He changed my life in so many ways, and I will always be grateful for that. His wife Helena was a beautiful, wise woman who accepted me and let me into her life. I did not keep in touch with them the way I wanted to. I suppose I thought they would always be here. Now I know that was the biggest mistake of my life. I would give anything to be able to pick up the phone and hear his voice. Jerry, thank you. I miss you." Now my voice was cracking, and there was no holding back. I was crying the kind of cry that comes from your gut. Trying to catch my breath, I walked off and sat down.

The minister spoke a few more words and read another Scripture that I barely heard, and then they played a sad hymn. I was in bad shape and unable to get up or speak. I had had so few people in my life that I cared about, and never anyone like Jerry. I loved him like a father and was experiencing this loss like a child.

Soon the church emptied except for me, Riley, Samantha, and their baby. We were still seated in silence. I looked at Samantha. I noticed she wasn't crying; instead, she had a sort of pissed-off look on her face. The baby was cutely wrapped in a blanket. He had been quiet the entire service. I looked up at Samantha again, smiled, and said, "He is a beautiful baby."

"Thanks," is all she said. I didn't get a good vibe from her; her bad energy hit me in waves, which was quite jarring considering my sorrow.

I stood up and looked at Riley. "Please let me know if I can help in any way." Then I walked to my car, feeling emptier and more alone than ever.

CHAPTER 48

HOPE

Two weeks later, I was still unable to function. I had not been to the office nor any appointments, and I hadn't even seen Austin. I was slipping into a depression. I knew I had to snap out of it but didn't know how.

On a Tuesday morning about two and a half weeks after the service, I was at home in my pajamas, just moping around. There was a knock on the door. A look out the peephole revealed Austin, and he was holding a beautiful bouquet.

Oh no! I look terrible... I thought about not answering, but I knew he knew I was home. I slowly opened the door. He didn't say anything, just wrapped his arms around me and held me. At first I tried to pull away, but he pulled me closer and hung on. So I gave in and the floodgates opened. He didn't speak as I sobbed; he just waited, and when I finally stopped he looked at me and said, "I am so sorry."

I was embarrassed, but it felt good to be so vulnerable in front of him. It was soothing in a way I had never experienced.

"How about if we go for a walk?"

"I guess, but I look terrible."

"You do, but let's go anyway."

We both laughed a little. As we stepped outside, I realized I had not had any sunshine in days. The fresh air felt good, and the breeze on my face was amazing. We walked and did not talk. At the end, Austin said, "I'm not leaving you alone, so would you like to come to my house?"

I paused. "Okay."

So we went over to his place. I went outside and sat in the backyard, which I'd always found to be so relaxing. He cooked fresh scallops and asparagus and opened a bottle of white Bordeaux, and we sat outside in silence. I realized I hadn't had an actual meal since the service. I have been snacking on whatever I found at home. After dinner, Austin asked me if I felt better.

"Yes I do, thank you."

"How is Jerry's son coping?"

"I don't know. He won't engage with me very much. I have offered to help, but he keeps saying no."

"Keep trying, he might need you later on. I guess he will sell the house they bought in Bel Air Estates?"

I hadn't thought of that at all. "Wow... yeah, he'll need to sell it unless they move into it and sell the other house." I thought about the beautiful home on Village Road. *Jerry and Helena loved that house. I'm glad they got to experience it, even if only for a short time. All this makes me realize that life is so fragile… We can have the best laid plans, and, the next minute, they fall apart.*

Seeing me deep in thought and worried my mood would sink again, Austin suggested we go in. I was so tired from the wine; for the past few weeks I hadn't been drinking and barely eating, so it went straight to my head.

"I think I am going to go lay down."

"Me too," he said. We went to Austin's bedroom, undressed, and got into bed, and he pulled me close. I drifted off to sleep quickly. It was the best night's sleep I had had in a long time.

The next morning, I felt like a new person. I had my coffee outside with Austin and then went for a run for the first time since the service. Then I took a shower and got dressed. I was feeling like me again—a heartbroken me, but nevertheless me.

CHAPTER 49

RAGE

I made up my mind to act as though I'd never met Blake Parker if I ever crossed paths with him again. I was definitely never answering any more calls. After that horrendous phone conversation, I was convinced he was the most arrogant ass I had ever met.

I had a busy day at the office. Around four, Chloe walked into my office and said, "Hey, do you want to grab a drink at Lulu's?"

"Sure. Let me send a quick email, and I'll be ready."

Chloe and I found seats at the bar and I ordered a martini while she got a glass of pinot noir. We talked about real estate. I'd grown fairly close to her.

After about an hour, Chloe excused herself to the ladies' room. A minute later I felt someone walk up behind me and touch my arm. I looked around and saw *him*.

I pulled away and jumped up from my seat. I was horrified. *What the hell is he doing here?!* Aloud I stated firmly, "I would like you to leave." My voice was a little louder than I intended, and several people glanced over.

Blake raised his eyebrows and smiled. "Wow, baby, that isn't very nice."

"Don't call me baby and get the fuck away from me!" It just came out, and very loudly.

Blake looked into my eyes. I saw fury deep inside. He didn't say a word more and walked away.

Chloe appeared at the bar. "Who was that hottie?"

"He's a dick!"

Chloe looked at me with surprise. I was visibly upset but tried to explain as briefly as possible. "It's a long story... He bought a listing of mine, and I made the mistake of having sex with him. He keeps hanging around and I can't seem to get rid of him."

Chloe looked out the window. "Um, that's him?"

I looked out the window. He was just sitting in his older model Cadillac, staring into the bar. I could make out his face. It was set angrily. "Yes, that's him. He's a freak."

Chloe smiled and commented, "Well, I didn't know you have sex with your freaky hot clients, or I may not have hired you." She was laughing. I tried to smile, but I was still shaken by the encounter.

CHAPTER 50
THE WILL

Finally feeling better, I went back to work. I started allowing myself to enjoy my home and my relationship with Austin. Yes, I still knew that I would eventually have to break it off; Elizabeth was still in the picture. But for now, I just wanted to enjoy how life was starting to feel somewhat normal again.

Monday morning, I decided to work from home and catch up. I was behind on paperwork for business and my bills. I was working in my office when my phone rang with a call from an unknown number.

"Paulina speaking."

The man who spoke had a deep and raspy voice. He sounded older. "Hello, is this Ms. Paulina Page?"

"Yes."

"My name is Robert Kline. I am with Kline and Hart Associates. I represent Mr. Jerry Newman's estate. Mr. Newman has identified you as part of his estate, and I would like to meet with you to discuss the details."

Just hearing Jerry's name made me feel weak. "His estate?" I repeated softly.

"Yes. Are you available to come into my office on Wednesday at 10 o'clock?"

"Um, okay, sure." I hung up, mind racing.

His estate? Maybe Jerry wanted me to do something for Riley? I tried not to think about it and went back to work.

On Wednesday, I woke up early and started to pace anxiously. I forced myself to eat—I managed to get one piece of wheat toast down and a cup of coffee. I arrived early and walked into the attorney's office. The place was drenched in rich, dark wood and moody lighting. The receptionist asked me to take a seat. Very soon a tall man in a navy blue suit walked around the corner, and we made eye contact. "Hello. Ms. Paige?"

I stood up. "Hello."

"Please come with me." We walked down a narrow hall into a large conference room and sat down. He began, "Mr. Newman was a longtime client of mine. He was also a friend."

My voice cracked as I said, "He was a friend of mine too."

He looked at me straight in the eye again and said, "I am sorry for your loss. I have some information for you." He lifted a large box from the floor and set it on the table, then he lifted a bronze metal box out of that box and placed it on the table. "This is for you. I will step out." He left.

I was alone in the conference room with the metal box. I slowly opened it and took a deep breath. On the top of the box was a sealed envelope, and under it was a stack of documents. I slowly opened the envelope. I recognized the handwriting right away as Jerry's, and for a moment I felt like he was still alive. The letter read:

Paulina,

If you are reading this letter, I have passed away. It is strange to write this to you when I am still alive, but as you know, I am a planner. The first time I spoke to you on the phone you were a young realtor at Remington Homes. I called to get information on purchasing some investment properties. You were courteous, sharp, and direct. I liked you from the start. The next day we met in person, and I knew from the first moment that you are an honest, hardworking person. What I didn't realize was that you would work around the clock for me, going above and beyond to find me the best investment properties on the market. In fact, to this day the properties you located for me are some of my best-performing investments. I always knew you were looking out for my best interest. I knew there was a fire in your soul to be successful. I knew you have a story to tell, and I sensed that it has to do with your upbringing. Whatever it is, I could always see that you have made your own way in this world through your own blood, sweat, and tears. You have earned everything you have by your own merit, and I respect that immensely. I have always felt like a father of sorts toward you and wanted to help you as much as I could. I was so proud of the way that you handled the negotiations on the house on Village Road. You were able to get us an excellent deal, and we love that house. Helena always says it has perfect feng shui.

Speaking of the house on Village Road—I leave it to you. There is a quitclaim deed attached, and you are the new owner. I genuinely believe that you belong in this home. There is a mortgage on the house, but it is small considering the price of the property. There is a significant amount of equity. I am asking a few things of you. Please honor these things in my name:

1. Do not ever sell this house. Live in it and enjoy it. The mortgage payment will be affordable if you keep working as you are now. I know you, and you like to work. Pay extra towards the principal every month.

2. Keep it in the name of a trust that you set up in your name only, even if you get married. If you have a child, leave the house to your child when you die.

3. Don't feel intimidated by the people in the neighborhood. You are just as intelligent, or more so, than all of them. What's more, you are kind.

4. Please watch over Riley however you can. He tends to close himself off to others, but over time he may need you to be there. Please keep offering your help.

5. Try to get to know Trevor. He will need a good role model. I don't think the marriage between Riley and Samantha will last, and he will need a respectable female role model and someone that he can trust. I don't know how old Trevor or Riley will be when you are reading this, but at any age, they will need you to be their friend and someone they can trust when Helena and I are gone.

I want you to know that I am proud of you. I respect you and love you as I would my own daughter. I know I never told you this in person, but I think you somehow just know. I hope so.

I wish you a healthy, happy life. I will see you on the other side. Until then.

God bless, Love, Jerry

I folded up the letter, held it to my heart, closed my eyes, and sent up a prayer to my friend. *Jerry, words cannot explain the gratitude I have for you. It's hard to believe that you have left me this incredible, life-changing gift. The truth is, though, you have been changing my life since the first time I met you. I will never underestimate nor forget what you have done for me. I promise to uphold your wishes and will do my best to get to know and help Riley and Trevor. Please watch over all of us. Thank you. I love you.*

There were tears in my eyes as I stared at the letter in my hand. When I said "I love you" in my prayer, it was the first time I had ever said those words to anyone. I felt faint.

I heard a knock on the door. In a weak voice I called, "Come in."

The attorney walked in and said, "Do you have any questions?"

"Is there anything I need to do?

"No, I will record the quitclaim deed today, and you will be the owner of the property."

Mr. Kline reached into the box and pulled out another envelope, a smaller one. He handed it to me saying, "Here is the key."

I held it in my hand for a moment, then stood up. As I left, I reached out and shook his hand. "Thank you."

I turned and walked out to my car, where I sat for about thirty minutes in silence. I was in shock. As I was parked there, I vaguely noticed a car pulling into the parking lot near me. I saw the faces of Riley and Samantha and quickly looked down; I felt strange and didn't want them to see me. They walked in the building, husband shuffling behind wife. That's when the obvious fact hit me: *Jerry left the house to me instead of Riley! Why?! Riley will have plenty of money with all of the other assets and the other house, but I hope he doesn't hold this against me...*

Now I had concern to add to my shock.

On the spur of the moment I decided to drive by the house on Village Road. As I drove into the neighborhood and gazed around, I thought to myself, *This can't be true. I don't belong here. I can never fit in.* I pulled up to the house and parked. The last time I was here was for the home inspection; both Jerry and Helena were here and alive. I would never have dreamed this would be my new reality. I parked and stared at the house and at the key in turns. I couldn't make myself go in. I couldn't do it. I drove away.

CHAPTER 51

THE MOVE

A few more days left me no less stunned to be the new owner of the house in Bel Air Estates. Jerry had given me specific instructions to reside there. Without question I accepted the move; I would honor every request he left me, no matter what.

Considering the contents of Jerry's letter, I decided the first thing I should do was talk to Riley. I dialed the number nervous and unsure what to say. Riley answered in a low voice.

"Hello."

I tried to sound upbeat and pleasant. "Hi Riley, this is Paulina. I just wanted to reach out and see how you are doing and if there is anything I can do to help right now?"

"No," he answered softly.

"Okay... I also wanted to talk to you about the house on Village Road. I don't know if you're aware that your father left the property to me. I hope this does not upset you. I was, and still am, shocked that he did so."

Riley was silent for a second and then replied, "It's okay, that's what he wanted to do."

I felt the tears starting again. "I haven't been in the house yet. I was hoping you would come with me to walk through and let me know which furniture or personal items you would like."

He quickly replied, "I don't want anything."

I was shocked. "I'm sure there must be something—pictures, furniture, something?"

"No, thank you. Goodbye, Paulina." He hung up.

I felt so discouraged; Riley had shut me out. Again. I knew that I had to go to the house, but I didn't want to go alone. So I called Austin.

"Hi, I have some big news."

"Big news?" He had a smile in his voice. "I can't wait to hear it."

"How about you meet me at my place?" I decided I would surprise him.

He laughed and said, "I can't wait, I am on my way!"

The idea of walking through Jerry's front door was almost too much to handle, and the fact that his house was now mine was getting more incomprehensible by the minute. My anxiety was rising. Luckily Austin was at my side within an hour. I met him outside and said,

"Come with me, I will drive." He looked surprised but got in my car without question. I was quiet as we were driving; I didn't even have the radio on.

After about ten minutes Austin spoke. "The suspense is killing me. Are you taking me to a secret location to seduce me?"

I looked at him with tears in my eyes, and in a low voice I said, "I'm taking you to the house at 18 Village Road. I need you to walk through it with me."

Austin could see my emotion. "No worries, darling, I'm with you."

We were silent the rest of the way. We pulled up in front of the house. It took me a few minutes to get out of the car. I opened the small white envelope and saw one key inside; my hand shook as I slowly unlocked the door. As we walked in, the first thing I noticed was a coffee cup on the kitchen table. It looked as if it had just been set there, and someone was coming back for it any minute. Photos of Jerry, Helena, and Riley covered the walls, and the painting I'd given them of the house was hanging in the sunroom. The sight brought a sob to my throat. I walked into the master bedroom and looked in the walk-in closet; all of their clothes were hanging neatly, and Helena's shoes filled an entire side. As I looked around, I had the feeling that they might walk in anytime. It was so eerie to think that they were never coming back.

Austin was standing on the deck looking at the view. When I walked out he turned and said, "Are you okay?"

With tears in my eyes I managed to say, "Yes."

"Will you be selling this home for them?"

"No, I will be living here."

Austin's jaw dropped. "What?"

I looked at the ocean and said, "This is my house. Jerry left it to me, and he asked me to live here, so that is what I am going to do."

He was quiet and then reached for me. He held me for a long time. "I will help you move. We're getting pretty good at it." He smiled that half smile I loved.

I kissed him. "Yes, please help me."

The next few weeks were a blur. I spent every day going through the rooms at Jerry's house. I carefully packed up all the framed photographs and wrapped them in bubble wrap. I packed all their clothes and personal belongings neatly in separate boxes and labeled them. There was also personal paperwork and an unlocked safe that contained some jewelry and cash. I took all of these items to Riley's house. I didn't call first, I just drove there. I buzzed the gate for entrance, and the gate opened. Samantha opened the front door and just stared at me without a word.

"Hi Samantha, is Riley here?"

"No, he is not. Can I help you?"

"Yes, I have some of Jerry and Helena's belongings, and I want Riley to have them. I know they would want it this way. If he does not wish to keep them, he can do whatever he chooses, but I need to leave them here. I will start unloading."

I did not wait for a response, I just started carrying the boxes to the front porch. Samantha opened the door wider and gestured into the foyer. "Just leave them in the front here." She did not offer to help.

I made eight trips, running out of breath before the end. When I set the last box down, she walked straight up to me and demanded, "Did you know that they completely cut me out of the will?"

After my initial surprise, I felt like saying, "Good!" But instead, I responded truthfully, "No, I didn't know that."

Samantha had a sneer to her voice. "It's hard to believe that they left you a house and me nothing. Last time I checked, you're just a real estate agent, I was their daughter-in-law. It is total bullshit! I am going to find a way around it!"

I almost slapped her on impulse. *What a spoiled little bitch!* With a deep breath, I tried to control myself. "You don't deserve anything. You are a taker, and Jerry and Helena despised takers. Also, I can assure you there is *not* a way around it."

I walked off with my heart pounding and blood boiling and a resolve to call Riley. He didn't answer, so I left a voicemail. "Riley, I dropped off some personal belongings of your parents at your house. They would have wanted you to have them. Samantha was there. I want you to know that I do not think she is looking out for your best interest. Maybe this is none of my business, but I need you to be aware of this. I am here if you need anything at all. Goodbye."

I kept some of the furniture and donated the rest, then moved into the house and rented out my townhome. The rental income would partially cover the mortgage on my new home. But I would still need a good income coming in every month to keep living there. I felt like I was over my head, but I kept hearing the words Jerry said in his letter. I would honor his wishes. I would open a trust in my name, and the property would be titled in the trust fund. I would never sell it. That was what Jerry had requested, and I would honor his wishes forever.

The neighbors were all curious about the new single woman who had bought the house on Village Road. No one knew that I was the realtor who had sold it to Jerry and Helena; in fact, no one knew a thing about me. I was a total mystery. There were rumors that I was a wealthy trust fund baby. Little did they know, I didn't belong there at all.

CHAPTER 52

IT NEVER LASTS

It was a dream living in the house on Village Road. I worked harder than ever and paid extra every month on the mortgage, just as Jerry had requested. As months flew by, it started to feel like home.

It was a hazy Thursday morning with a slight breeze, and seagulls were circling overhead. I was sitting outside with my coffee. Sometimes when I sat out on the deck, I felt like Jerry was there with me, watching over me. I was safe out there over the water in his presence. My mind drifted to Austin. It was hard to believe we had been dating for several years now. I was crazier than ever about him, but still knew it couldn't last. Elizabeth was still working with him, but they rarely traveled together anymore. There had been so much going on in my life, so I decided just to let it go. I knew that I was in love with Austin but was scared to death to admit it. In my heart, I still truly believed that love was impermanent by nature. So I did my best to keep my distance, which got more difficult every day.

We did not have any plans for the weekend yet, but we spent every weekend together, so I didn't give it much thought. I kept busy working all day and, exhausted, fell asleep by nine. The next morning, I was on the phone for hours. After lunch, I checked my phone and realized I had not heard from Austin, which was unusual since we talked or texted every day. Today was Friday, and we still did not have any plans for the weekend.

I was going to text him, but then decided to drive by his office instead. I don't know why; it was a spontaneous decision. A block from his office, I saw him sitting outside on a restaurant patio. We'd eaten there before; it was a trendy place with a great outdoor ambiance. He was sitting across from a woman with blonde hair in a short black skirt and high heels. I didn't know her. She looked sexy, and they were laughing together.

At once my heart sank. I felt like someone kicked me in the stomach and knocked the breath out of me. I quickly turned so they wouldn't see me and drove away as fast as I could. My heart was pounding and tears were falling. *That bastard! I knew it.* I just kept repeating it: *I knew it. I knew this would happen eventually. I am so stupid! So stupid!*

I went back home and paced back and forth. At four, Austin texted me, *Hi darling, Come on over and we can go for a spin on the water. I miss you. Kisses.* I deleted the text and turned off my phone. I suddenly felt almost numb; it was a feeling I remembered from childhood. I would just "switch off" and become completely emotionally numb. I had never felt that way before with Austin, but now I was completely resolved to let him go and move on. I went to bed at ten and did not recheck my phone. Just like that, I decided it was over.

Austin called me the next morning and texted twice more. *Darling, are you okay?* I did not respond at all. I felt so distant, like I had shut a door and locked it. I'd learned this ability as a child; back then, I had to learn how to cope, and feeling sorry for myself was not the answer.

On Sunday he knocked on my front door and I answered.

"Yes?"

He looked confused. "Are you okay? I have been trying to reach you all weekend."

"I'm fine, Austin. Look, I know about the girl, and it's okay. I don't ever want to see you again. Please pack up my things at your house and I will pick them up tomorrow. Leave them on the porch."

"What girl? What are you talking about?"

"I saw you with the blonde at lunch. I am not an idiot. Please leave."

"Wait, that girl is a client. She invested $4 million with me. I took her to lunch, that's it!"

I was sweating. "I don't believe you. Get out!"

Austin looked hurt and confused. "You're making a mistake, Paulina! I love you and I would never cheat on you."

I was starting to cry but was determined that he would not see it. "Get out!"

Austin slowly turned and walked away.

I cried myself to sleep that night. I refused to answer his calls or texts and texted him only once the next day to ask him again to leave my clothes that were at his house out on the porch. When I went by to pick them up, he opened the door. He looked like he might have been starting to cry as he asked, "Can we talk?" I said no tersely, grabbed my things, and left.

I did not speak to Austin again.

CHAPTER 53

FEAR

I had become a very successful real estate agent. Once I had started networking with my neighbors in Bel Air Estates, working on a referral basis became my way of life. I had not dated anyone since Austin. The pain was deep, but I was at peace with it. After all, he could not be trusted.

I drove home after happy hour with Chloe, still shaken from running into Blake. I was surprised how loud and strong my voice had been at the bar. I drove back home and locked the door behind me. It had been over a year now, and Blake had still not moved into the house on Tortoiseshell Drive. The exterior was deteriorating, the lawn was suffering, and the shades were heavy with dust. It was all so strange.

I put together a salad for dinner and poured a glass of Chardonnay, and then took it outside on the deck. As I ate, I wondered whether Jerry had loved this spot as much as I did. After dinner, I went downstairs to the theatre room to watch a movie. Even though I'd seen *Pretty Woman* multiple times, I only loved it more each time. I cried at the end, as was my custom.

I checked all the doors in the basement as I always did to make sure everything was locked up. Upstairs on the main level I checked the doors as well, then retired to my room. I loved my place. I had it decorated just the way I liked, with light blue and white colors and a comfortable beachy vibe. Climbing into bed, I picked up my favorite personal development book. I turned off the light after a while and fell asleep thinking about Austin. He had tried to reach me several times, but I never responded. I still thought about him almost every night and ached for his arms around me in sleep. I didn't expect to ever let anyone in again.

I woke up abruptly in the middle of the night. The room was pitch black; I could never sleep if there was even a dim nightlight nearby. My first thought was that someone was in my bedroom. I sensed eyes looking at me. I bolted upright and peered around from under my blankets. I didn't see anything or anyone, so I shook my head clear, telling myself that I'd just had a bad dream. I turned over in bed and tried to get comfortable again. But I got the same feeling again, and it crept over my skin. I rolled over and looked towards the hall, and there was the outline of someone standing in the doorway motionlessly, looking at me. I screamed louder than I have ever screamed in my entire life.

The outline didn't move; it just stood there, silent and staring. I jumped out of bed on the far side and screamed again, as ear-splittingly as I could. But I knew that no one would hear me. The house sat up on a bluff and there were not any others close enough. The knowledge that no one was able to hear my cries for help was terrifying.

The person remained still as a statue, but I felt the hostility radiating towards me. My eyes swiveled around the room, searching for anything to defend myself with. My phone was in my office, and the security alarm was off. I never slept with it at night. The thought of grabbing the lamp and throwing it crossed my mind—but then the person started towards me, almost in a casual saunter. I was confused, terrified, and frozen in place; my heart was pounding so hard, I thought I was having a heart attack. As the person came slowly closer, I recognized the shape as a man's. And as he got within a few feet, I saw Blake. I screamed again and tried to rush past him. I pushed him aside with all my strength, but he just grabbed me and held my arms behind my back. His body was pressed against mine, and I could see his face now. His eyes were full of rage. He looked like a monster. He did not say a word, just dragged me from the bedroom. When we reached the kitchen he turned on the light, still holding my arms tightly behind my back. He glared at me with the darkest look in his eyes I had ever seen. Even worse than my father.

He pulled me close and said, "Now you're going to play it my way. Do you hear me, you little bitch?" I was petrified; he was stronger than me, and I felt helpless. I tried to breathe but was hyperventilating too hard. My mind raced. A voice in my head said, *Trick him.* It was a soft, calm, still voice. I was trying to catch my breath, and my heart was pounding so hard I could barely hear the words. Then it spoke again, more clearly: *Trick him.*

I somehow managed to speak. "Hi Blake, it's nice to see you."

Blake jerked me around hard and spat, "That's not what you said earlier today, bitch. I have a plan for you. I have wanted to finish my fantasy with you for a long time, and tonight is the night." He gave an evil laugh.

I tried my hardest to sound calm. "Let's have some fun. You don't have to be so rough."

He looked at me and sneered, "I like it rough."

I waited a minute until I could speak again and said, "How about if we have some wine?"

He loosened his grip and considered, examining my face. "Okay baby. Maybe we can have some fun."

My body was shaking and my thoughts were tumbling. I scanned the room for a weapon as I turned to open the wine fridge. I pulled out a bottle of red wine and handed it to Blake saying, "Can you open it?" He found a wine opener in a drawer. I noticed it had a sharp edge and thought about stabbing him in the eye with it, but decided that plan wasn't good enough; he would overpower me, and then it would be all over. Blake poured us both a glass and seemed to be calming down a little.

I took a sip, then looked at him and said, "Blake, what do you have in mind for tonight?' I tried to sound composed. "Listen, I *am* attracted to you. I think that's been clear since the day we met. I'm sorry we got off on the wrong foot."

Blake debated with his head cocked to the side, looking me up and down. I realized I wasn't wearing anything under my thin nightgown. I felt a shiver go up my spine. I had no idea what I was going to do, but one thing I did know was that I was going to go down fighting. I would not just roll over.

With the most disgusting look on his face, he undressed me with his eyes, and then in a condescending voice he replied, "Well, we're going to go to my new house, back to the game room, and we are going to repeat the scene that we shared before. I've been dreaming about it since it happened. The furniture is still there, and everything is in place just as it was before. I can't wait to bend you over the couch again." He laughed.

I felt like I was going to pass out. *He is planning to take me to that house and rape me.* I started praying, *Dear God, please help me. Please get me out of this. Please.* I forced a fake laugh as I gripped the countertop tightly. I am not sure where the words came from, but a voice that did not sound like mine suggested, "How about if we relax here in my game room and have some more wine, and then we will go to your house and relive our encounter?" I was buying time—for what, I had no idea.

Blake smiled and pulled me close into a kiss. I almost gagged; it took all my strength not to pull away and hit him. It was not the right time yet.

After we kissed, I refilled his glass with a smile. I wanted to get him drunk, or at least buzzed, to throw him off his game. When he turned his back, I poured mine in the sink and then pretended to be drinking it. Blake picked out another bottle and seemed to be relaxing. I kept praying, *Please God, show me what to do. Please.* We went downstairs together, and I turned on some music. "Would you like to play pool?" I asked.

Blake smiled. "Sure, baby." He was downing the wine now and seemed to be getting tipsy. As he started to set up the game, I said, "Excuse me, I have to go to the ladies' room," and walked down the downstairs hall towards the bathroom.

My brain was in overdrive. I spun circles in the hall, desperately trying to think of a way out. But there were no exits on this side of the house; the closest was the door in the main room, where Blake was. I ran into the storage room. There was a large closet in there where I had never really explored; there were still some of Jerry's things stored inside. My heart felt like it would jump out of my chest. I wrapped my arms around myself, trying to calm down enough to think clearly. Then I saw the gun safe.

I remembered the day Jerry and I stood in this room and I asked him whether he wanted to keep the safe. Oddly, I had never looked inside of it since moving in. I'd forgotten about it completely. I knew I was running out of time; I looked at the safe and thought, *It is probably locked, or empty.* I quickly pulled the handle and to my surprise, it was open, and there were several guns inside. Two were rifles, and one was a small handgun.

I had never shot a gun before. I flashed back to a childhood scene where my father stood in the bedroom brandishing a pistol with evil in his eyes, while my mom hovered in the corner crying wordlessly. I remember thinking that she was simply waiting to die. I was around seven at the time, and it felt like I was right there again.

I grabbed the handgun. I didn't even know if it was loaded or how to use it, but it was the only chance I had.

Blake's voice drifted into the storage room. "Where are you, baby? I am ready to play," he laughed. He walked around the corner, and I was standing there holding the gun. Shock flew across his face, and then he quickly smiled and said, "Put that down, baby, before someone gets hurt." He took a step towards me.

I pointed the gun at him and pulled the hammer back like I'd seen in movies. I had no real idea what I was doing; it happened so fast. He stopped for a second and said, "Now come on baby, we both know you are not the type of broad that would shoot someone."

I looked him directly in the eyes and warned, "*Take one more step, and you're a dead man.*" I was shaking so badly I could barely hold the gun up.

He laughed, "So we *are* going to have to play rough, then? I will have to take the gun from you and spank you with it. You need to be disciplined for being such a bad girl." He started towards me.

I aimed at his chest, closed my eyes, and pulled the trigger. The thunder filled my ears. The bullet hit him directly in the chest. He fell to the ground, and blood was suddenly everywhere. I stumbled past him and up the stairs, hysterically screaming and crying. I grabbed my phone from my office on the way out the door, then sprinted down the street, barefoot and in my nightgown. I ran as fast as I could to the house closest to me, jumped onto the porch, punched the doorbell repeatedly, and then fell to the ground sobbing. I didn't know the neighbors Kathy and Harold well; we had seen each other at parties and waved to each other when we got our mail.

Kathy opened the door after a minute or so—I couldn't say exactly how much time passed—and looked horrified at the sight of me. I realized I still had the gun in my hand. I wept, "Please help, please call the police." Then Kathy stepped back and Harold appeared in her place. "Oh my god, are you okay? Come in! Please!"

I crawled through the door and lay on the floor with the pistol in one hand and my phone in the other. Kathy and Harold both stood back and stared at me, immobile in shock. I looked at my phone, and without thinking, dialed Austin's number. It had been a couple of years but I recalled the digits perfectly.

Austin answered after a few rings, his voice hesitating. "Paulina?"

All I could say was, "Help me, please." I could barely get the words out.

"Where are you?"

"I am at my neighbor's house. I just killed a man." I hung up and lay there on the floor. My mind drifted from consciousness.

I was shaken back to reality by the sound of sirens outside. Then I felt someone crouch beside me on the floor. I looked up to see Austin's face. I reached for him, and he gathered me in more tightly than he'd ever held me before. We both cried and rocked each other. I held on for dear life. I felt like as long as he had his arms around me, I would be okay.

A police officer walked in the door. When he saw the state I was in, he went back to his squad car and returned with gloves on and a plastic bag. He asked me calmly to hand over the weapon. I slowly reached up and gave it to him, still clinging to Austin. The officer helped me up and asked me where I lived. I told him.

"I shot a man. He's in my basement. His name is Blake Parker."

The officer introduced himself as Matt and got straight to the point. "Are you sure he is still there? Did you kill him?"

The thought was terrifying—*Maybe he lived?* I could barely speak. "I am not sure… I shot him once, and he fell to the floor."

"We are going into the property. Please come with me to my car, we will have to take you in for questioning."

I looked at Austin and said, "I love you." It came without hesitation or any thought at all. I loved him. It was simple.

He looked at me with tears in his eyes and said, "I love you. I never stopped loving you."

I let go of his hand and walked to the police car. I sat and waited there for what seemed like forever. Soon an ambulance and more squad cars roared up the road towards my house.

CHAPTER 54

SAFETY

In shock and barely able to open my mouth, I felt as though my life was over. The squad car pulled in to the station and parked. I had no idea if Blake was dead or alive; all I knew was that my life would never be the same, and I would never be okay again.

I sat in the backseat staring blankly out the window. My hair was stringy, my eyes were so red they were almost swollen shut, and my bare feet were filthy and cut up from my run down the street. My wrists were rubbed raw and bruised from the way I'd been dragged through my house.

Matt opened the car door and said, "Please come with me." He held on to my arm as we went inside. There he asked me if I wanted some water or coffee.

I replied, "Water please," in a soft voice.

After going through what happened in detail, they said I was free to go home but could not travel out of the state or out of the country. I was afraid to ask, but I did anyway: "Is he dead?"

Matt looked at me and stated, "He's in intensive care. We don't know if he will make it out yet."

I couldn't speak. I didn't know what to do. How could I go back to my house? There was blood everywhere, and I was terrified to be alone. But when I was offered a ride home, I accepted, not having any other choice. I stood outside the station to wait and prayed, *Dear God, thank you for saving my life. Please help me again. I don't know what to do or where to go.*

I had my eyes closed and hands to my face as I wept. Then I felt someone walk up and wrap their arms around me. I knew right away it was Austin. I turned and fell into his embrace. He quietly said, "Come on, let's go home." I walked with him to his car and he drove me to his house.

I had not been there in so long. When we walked in, I noticed he had moved things around and bought some new furniture pieces. Austin simply led me to the master bathroom and said gently, "Why don't you take a shower. I don't have any clothes for you, but you can wear one of my t-shirts." I got in the shower and tried not to think about what had just happened, and when I got out he had left a t-shirt for me. I slipped it on and walked into the empty bedroom. So many memories of us came to mind, and I realized how badly I had missed him. I climbed into bed and quietly cried. Soon he came in and got into bed next to me. He held me all night, and I had no desire to move another muscle ever again. I felt like I could make it through this as long as he was with me.

The next morning I woke up feeling sore all over. My body and head ached. Austin was not there, so I got up and walked into the kitchen. He was cooking breakfast. He turned and smiled. "Good morning."

I tried to smile and said a hoarse "Hi." He handed me a cup of coffee and I walked outside and sat down. The backyard was as beautiful as I remembered.

The next minute he brought a vegetable omelet and some fresh fruit out. I managed to take a few bites. We were both quiet for a while, but Austin finally spoke.

"I am so sorry about what happened, darling. When you're ready to talk about it, I'm here. I'm so happy that you called me. I've waited for your call every day since you left. This isn't how I wanted the call to be, obviously, but I am still glad… to see you again."

I knew with all my heart that I loved Austin more than anything and that I never wanted to be apart again. But the only words that came out were, "Me too." He did not pressure me for details about anything. I stayed at his house, unable to think of going back to mine.

CHAPTER 55

TRUTH

After three days of Austin's comforting presence, I was still in shock but starting to feel a little bit better. He took off from work to be with me. I had not heard anything from Matt in that time, nor had I been back to my house. I knew I would have to go eventually, but for now, I was so grateful to be where I was. At 9:00 a.m. on the third day, my phone rang. I didn't recognize the number.

"Hello, Paulina speaking."

"Hello, Paulina. This is Matt with the LAPD. I need you to come down to the station for a few more questions."

I felt my heart skip a beat. "Okay, when?"

"Today around noon would be good."

"Okay, can I ask you a question?"

"Yep."

"Is Blake alive?"

"Yes, he is. He is still in the hospital and will most likely have some ongoing issues from the wound, but it appears he will live."

The words took my breath away. *He will live.* I mustered my strength to say, "Okay," and hung up. *What if I go to jail?! I did shoot a man, after all!*

When Austin came in, I expressed this thought out loud. "What if I get charged for killing him? He is going to live! ...That son of a bitch is going to live."

Austin assured me calmly, "He assaulted you in your own home. It was self-defense."

"I have to go talk to the police today."

"Okay, I will go with you."

By the time we got to the station, I was so worked up that I could barely contain myself. *Why am I being questioned, when this bastard tried to rape and most likely kill me? I should have shot him twice!*

Matt greeted me. Once I shook his hand, I got right to the point. "If I am going to be questioned, then I will need an attorney. This man broke into my home and tried to rape and kill me, and now I feel like I'm the criminal."

Matt replied with perfect composure, "You are not being questioned for a crime. No charges are placed against you. Paulina, we have been tracking Mr. Parker for several years. He is a suspect for money laundering, and now the illegal growing of marijuana as well."

"What?" I replied, confused.

"We have searched the house he purchased on Tortoiseshell Drive. The entire place is set up as a very extensive, high-end grow house. The only room that is not being used is the rec room. He has been trying to buy other homes in the area to use for the same purpose. He targeted your neighborhood because no one would suspect it, it's too upscale. He has a business partner, a young lady named Chelsea McCarthy. Mr. Parker was one of the first investors in Bitcoin, and we suspect that he has purchased millions of dollars' worth of real estate and drugs with Bitcoin. The property on Tortoiseshell is the only property he has bought with U.S. currency, and that's how we traced him as the owner. He will be on trial for multiple charges, including the attack against you, once released from the hospital... I do have a question for you regarding the entry of your home, Paulina. There was no sign of forced entry. Did Mr. Parker ever get a key to your home?"

I quickly said, "Of course not!" But then it hit me—*Blake lived there with the previous owner Thomas Weaver... he probably had a key!* As a realtor, I always tell my clients to change the locks when they buy a house. That had to be it.

When I shared this, Matt said they will be looking at the evidence to see if Blake had a key to the property on his person. Matt took off his glasses he looked tired he looked up at me and said, "You are free to go, but you will need to testify, so do not to leave the state or country." He assured me that Blake would not be free on bail and that I did not need to worry about going home.

I walked out of the police station, and Austin was waiting on a bench. I ran to him and hugged him. I decided right there to put my heart on the line.

"I love you so much! I am so sorry that I pushed you away... I was afraid of getting hurt and when I saw you with that blonde woman, I panicked. I was constantly expecting that you would find someone better than me and it would end between us, so I ended it first. There are things about my past that I have never told you. I am afraid that you will not want to be with me when you learn about my childhood and my family. I've lied to you, I am not as I appear to be."

Tears sprang to his eyes as he listened, but he reacted quickly. "I don't care about your past or your childhood. I love you. But you hurt me; you broke my heart. Can I trust you not to do that again?"

"Yes, I promise. Austin, I have never loved anyone before. I don't even know how to love anyone. But if you give me another chance, I will spend the rest of my life learning how to show you how much I love you. I never stopped thinking about you and I missed you every day."

He took my hand without another word, and we walked to his car. He helped me in and got into the driver's seat.

"We should go to your house. You don't have to stay there, but we need to go in."

I felt panic in my chest, but I knew he was right. "Okay," I replied.

We pulled up to the house, and I realized I didn't even have my key. We entered through the garage keypad. As we entered the kitchen, I saw the empty wine bottle and opener sitting on the countertop. I pictured the way Blake drank the wine and laughed. We walked into the bedroom, and I flashed back to seeing him standing on the threshold. Austin took my hand and said, "It's okay." We continued walking through the house and then down to the basement. There was a half-empty bottle of wine sitting on the table, and the pool table was set up ready to play. I slowly walked around the corner to the storage room and saw blood all over the carpet. It was smeared all over, as if he had dragged himself along the carpet trying to get up and leave. I started to cry and ran out of the room. Austin looked though the rest of the basement and said, "Okay, we can go, darling. I'll make sure they do not need any more evidence here, and then I will have the carpet replaced and the entire house professionally cleaned."

We walked out of the house. I stopped and stood in the front yard looking at the house. I suddenly knew that Jerry had been there that night. He had led me to the safe. He had left the guns there, loaded, for my protection. Jerry and the grace of God saved my life.

CHAPTER 56

FATE

I knew that I was forever changed, that I'd been redefined as a person by that night. The trial would be starting soon. Hopefully, Blake and Chelsea would be going to prison for a very long time. And I had another chance with Austin. I was determined to get it right this time.

I sometimes wondered why certain things happen to some people and not to others. Why do some people live charmed lives, getting everything they want and more than they could ever need, almost as if God is smiling on them; while others struggle through each day and endure pain and hardship? After what I experienced, I came to believe that we are all here to learn specific lessons that are unique to us as individuals, and that these lessons teach us exactly what we need to learn.

When I felt strong enough, I returned to my house alone. I went out to the deck and looked at the horizon. A seagull flew directly over me and began slowly circling around and around above my head.

I knew in my heart it was a sign from Jerry letting me know I would be okay. I wiped away the tears in my eyes, looked out at the waves, and smiled.

The End

A MESSAGE FROM THE AUTHOR

Thank you for reading The Secrets That Follow I hope you enjoyed it. The story for this book came to me on a random Saturday morning. The characters quickly become close to my heart, I love Paulina's spirit and her unyielding determination to find a better life for herself. Paulina reminds us that regardless of our background and the obstacles we face we can live the life we dream of if we believe we can and refuse to give up.

Though this book came to a close I know Paulina has more of her story to share with us. Stay tuned.

Paula Marie

Author

Made in the USA
Monee, IL
02 June 2020

32395973R00138